CURLY CLIX CONVICTIONS

Narghiza Ergashova

Table of Contents

Enrico's 46th Birthday Party 1

The Beginning of a Story Worth Telling 3

A Side Note On Success 6

Enrico's 46th Birthday Party 8

The Anatomy of Betrayal and Abuse 11

The Gaslighting, Abuse and Manipulation 34

Enrico's 46th Birthday Party 45

Final Cohabitation Attempt 48

Enrico's 46th Birthday Party 52

The Plan: After the Final Cohabitation Attempt Fails 55

The Plan: The Wedding 73

The Plan: After The Wedding 77

Who am I? 89

Journey to Healing 95

Enrico's Recollection of The Day snd Events After 108

Curly Clux Convictions 115

Enrico's 46ᵗʰ Birthday Party

Set on the 43rd floor of the luxury apartment complex at 101 Bathurst Street, Sydney CBD, Enrico's Gatsby-inspired 46th birthday party was the epitome of opulence and celebration. From the moment guests arrived, they were meant to feel as though they had stepped into a world of glamour - one that promised sophistication and indulgence in equal measure. The atmosphere was anchored by a grand brown-and-gold décor wall, a backdrop that framed the rusty brown and gold five-tier cake, surrounded by helium balloons drifting softly in place. That first impression lingered, setting the tone for a night designed to be extravagant and memorable.

The balcony had been transformed into a mobile mini-bar, where a barman served an array of drinks with practiced ease. Inside, the spread was as rich as expected - decadent hors d'oeuvres, caviar stations, and a dessert bar lined with macarons and champagne-infused cupcakes, each one a small piece of indulgence that delighted guests as much as the view.

For something more playful, more alive, there were the Latin dancers. They didn't just perform - they became part of the evening's rhythm, taking to the floor twice an hour. And after every set, they would reach out, inviting the guests in, turning watchers into dancers, and pulling everyone a little deeper into the celebration.

Enrico's 46th wasn't just a party. It was built to be something more - a night where the lines blurred between spectacle and experience.

And I wasn't just the host.

I was the one behind it all. The director, the planner, the one who had imagined it and then watched it take shape, piece by piece. I stood there, caught between the thrill of seeing it come to life and the quiet panic of watching small things slip just out of reach.

Narghiza Ergashova and Enrico Pucci, 2019 – Bali, Indonesia

The Beginning of a Story Worth Telling

It began in February 2018, when Enrico and I first connected through Facebook. He initiated the conversation by sending me a promotional message about his business, GPSFM, detailing its offerings on Facebook Messenger. At first, I was intrigued. Facebook Messenger seemed like the wrong platform for promotions of this sort, yet Enrico came across as someone with a clear enthusiasm for building connections.

After accepting his invitation, Enrico persistently reached out, expressing his genuine desire to meet in person and explore potential avenues for cooperation. His follow-ups were tactful yet determined. Eventually, his persistence paid off, and I agreed to speak with him. At the time, I was working in a technical, financial accounting role, where my responsibilities were largely confined to strict adherence to accounting standards and meticulous reporting. The nature of my work left little room for entrepreneurial experimentation, and I doubted I had much to contribute. Nevertheless, I decided to call Enrico to discuss his proposal, choosing to reach out through a private number.

The conversation felt like a job interview but far more expansive, delving into my personal life in a way that teetered on the edge of intrusive without crossing into outright creepiness. The curiosity was palpable. I instinctively sensed that Enrico wasn't interested in doing business with me; his interest ran much deeper than that.

At the time I met Enrico, I was already emotionally detached from my marriage to Damon Samuel Rockwell. The marriage had long since devolved into a hollow, imbalanced partnership. Damon had gone bankrupt twice during our ten-year relationship. It took him years to recover from the first bankruptcy and become eligible for basic things like a credit card or to apply for a home or personal loan. But once discharged, he wasted no time, jumping into another business, racking up debts, and once again falling into a second bankruptcy. The key was that he could afford to go repeatedly into and out of bankruptcy. He had a migrant working horse, Narghiza Ergashova, at home, holding his lifestyle together while he spent ten years experimenting with his non-existent business skills.

The emotional toll of Damon's inability to enter any financial partnership with me or sustain his own living expenses weighed heavily, but it also served as a catalyst for the change I so desperately sought.

My situation seemed untenable. I turned my focus toward gaining financial independence - an essential step in the path toward filing for divorce. I began quietly strategizing, taking on extra responsibilities at work, and seeking out new avenues for professional growth that could provide both stability and a safety net. Money, or the lack of it, had always been a central point of tension in our marriage, and I refused to allow financial dependency to become a barrier to my freedom. This was not just about practical preparation; it was about reclaiming a sense of agency that had been dulled for far too long.

It happened on the 6th of April 2018. Damon moved out. Though expected, moving out and coming back with an ultimatum was a classic Damon Rockwell move; his absence stretched into two and a half weeks, leaving me in a state of hope that this time he wouldn't come back, nor would I accept his conditions. But he did come back. As it turned out, the grandstanding gesture had been a trip to our undercover car park in the apartment complex where we lived, where he stayed in his Toyota four-wheel drive the entire time, and then returned to my apartment, trying to reconcile with me.

The reunion was anything but peaceful. Damon's demeanour was desperate yet resolute as he pleaded for reconciliation, expressing a fervent desire to repair the fractures in our marriage. Our conversations were intense, and so were the offers laid on the table: Damon was willing to disown his own mother - she had caused friction in our relationship from the very beginning. He was willing to cut ties with his troubled eldest daughter. Yet the train for those compromises had long since left. For me, the answer was still "no."

Damon moved out again on the 18th of April 2018. That date became our final separation date.

A Side Note On Success

Success, by its very nature, possesses an alluring quality that can become deeply addictive. The captivating power of achievement lies in its ability to trigger a potent psychological response, activating the brain's reward circuitry through the release of dopamine. This biochemical reinforcement compels individuals not only to seek further success but also to tie their sense of identity and self-worth to these achievements.

Within romantic partnerships, this dynamic often extends to partners who begin to derive their own sense of fulfillment and pride from the success of the other. Research in social psychology highlights that romantic relationships involve intricate systems of emotional and cognitive interdependence. When one partner achieves success - whether professionally, academically, or socially - the other often shares in that validation, forging a shared identity built around the dynamic of achievement. Over time, this vicarious reliance on another's success can create a feedback loop of emotional dependency. And post-separation, many find themselves unable to untangle their self-perception from their partner's achievements. This inability to "let go" isn't simply an emotional attachment - it can be seen as a form of psychological addiction, the mind clinging to the rewards once gained from sharing in someone else's success.

It's November 2012, and I'm a residential year student at AGSM. During a lecture, a PhD freshman introduces a concept with a decision tree-like diagram. He explains that the more successful a business's intellectual property (IP) becomes, the more likely it is to face legal battles. Skeptical, I raise my hand, convinced the idea is flawed. I argue that if the IP is solid, failsafe, and properly patented, there should be little opportunity for others to challenge it. I question the notion that greater success inevitably attracts litigation.

He listens, then explains: it's about the benefits derived from litigation. The greater the benefit to be gained, the more opportunists will try. After all, no one sues a business with nothing to offer. His perspective reframes my understanding - success doesn't just attract customers. It attracts challengers. People who want their share. Competitors who sue for similar IP, claiming they came up with it first. Communities seeking damages because a business asset blocks their view.

The more success, the more opportunistic behaviour.

Enrico's 46th Birthday Party

Opulence has a price.

I was the one who paid it.

I originally planned for the performers to do a Michael Jackson impersonation, complete with his iconic dance moves. It reminded me of Shirina's 12th birthday party years ago, when we brought in a performer to teach us the choreography for "Thriller."

That party was an absolute success, thanks in large part to the hilarious sight of parents trying - and failing - to keep up with their kids during the dance class. They looked like uncoordinated logs, completely out of rhythm, and I remember laughing so hard I was literally rolling on the floor. I wasn't much better at the moves myself, but I had to stop trying because the laughter overtook me. It was pure, unforgettable chaos.

Enrico wanted something different - entertainment that was captivating yet gentler. Something more sensual, more relatable, something that would resonate with his guests. After some brainstorming, we decided on a Latin theme.

My role was to handle every detail: sourcing the performers, booking the band, liaising with their manager, coordinating the shows, approving costumes, and reviewing their past performances. There was a lot to get done.

By mid-January 2022, everything was set.

The band was booked and paid for, and preparations were well underway to bring Enrico's vision for his 46th birthday celebration to life. It was shaping up to be a night to remember - live music, dazzling Latin dancers in tantalizing costumes, and an atmosphere of pure luxury.

The celebration created quite a buzz, with Enrico's friends and acquaintances eagerly anticipating the event.

Months later, the party - and those Latin dances - hit the news. Public curiosity turned quickly to scepticism. Questions swirled about how someone entangled in financial troubles could afford such extravagance. The stories painted a picture of indulgence and excess, questioning how Enrico's lavish lifestyle and opulent events were funded despite his string of bankruptcies. Yet what no one realized, beneath the noise of the rumours, was that every detail of that celebration - from the dancers to the last dime - was entirely funded by his wife, Narghiza Ergashova.

One of the most prominent reporters who covered his birthday was Janet Fife-Yeomans from News Corp Australia, Daily Telegraph. Her headlines featured my name, Narghiza Pucci, under a photo of me with Enrico on the beach at Byron Bay - a photo taken in December 2021. Of course, I didn't know that until late April 2022.

In late April, I received a frantic call from Ross Pucci, Enrico's brother. He sounded angry.

"Have you seen the latest edition of the Daily Telegraph?" he demanded.

I told him I hadn't.

"You are in it," he said.

Ross was livid, cursing the world and railing against what Enrico had allegedly done to their family. As I listened, I couldn't help but consider the psychological inflictions at play - how someone could deflect responsibility so completely, refusing to see their own faults, spiralling instead into denial and projection. I always knew brothers could be fiercely competitive, but the depth of that rivalry became clear to me over the weeks that followed, from late April to late May 2022.

By the end of May, I had secured an Apprehended Violence Order against Ross.

Indeed, Janet Fife-Yeomans' article surfaced in mid-April 2022.

By late September, she had edited my images and references out of her articles. Janet had compelling reasons to do so.

Narghiza Ergashova and Enrico Pucci, 2022 – Sydney, Australia. Images from Enrico's 46th Birthday

The Anatomy of Betrayal and Abuse

To understand high-conflict relationships, one must explore the anatomy of betrayal and abuse.

One of the most striking illustrations of deeply psychological abuse can be found in the metaphor of the frog in boiling water. If a frog is dropped into boiling water, it will instinctively jump out, recognizing the immediate danger. But if that same frog is placed in lukewarm water, and the heat is turned up slowly, it won't notice the rising temperature - until it's too late. This analogy captures how manipulation unfolds, not in grand gestures but in gradual, almost invisible steps. Small, seemingly harmless actions pile up until the shift is no longer subtle. By the time the true extent of the control becomes clear, the individual is often too deeply entrenched, too exhausted to escape. What once felt like small compromises now feel like chains, and the way out seems almost impossible.

The Player

From early 2018 to mid-2019, my relationship with Enrico flourished. We shared undeniable chemistry on many levels. He was easy-going, an all-rounder-relatable gentleman, and our mutual passion for business created a strong bond between us. We travelled; we celebrated every day, each other and everyone around us. He seemed to get along with my kids, Shirina and Kamron. We didn't just go through the motions - we genuinely lived.

Enrico and I travelled to Singapore for business and enjoyed a holiday in Bali a few months later. Each trip left us with unforgettable memories - new adventures, exciting places, and experiences unlike anything we had done before.

There were a few unexpected hiccups along the way, though. For instance, Belinda Pucci, Enrico's ex-wife, called me out of the blue and dropped a bombshell: she claimed they had been living together until just two weeks ago and were still married. She delivered this shocking revelation in a single breath before abruptly hanging up. Stunned and confused, I tried calling her multiple times to get some clarity, but my calls wouldn't go through. It quickly became clear - she had blocked me immediately after making that call. Enrico kindly explained that this was Belinda's signature move since their divorce - prank calls and out-of-this-world accusations.

I had no reason not to believe Enrico, but just to be sure, I asked for a copy of the divorce certificate. I had to remind him several times to send it through, and when he finally did, the PDF file attached was too large to open. I didn't want to sound petty beyond that point, so I left it at that. I genuinely believed Enrico was divorced.

Then, there was an incident where I lost access to my Facebook account on my phone. To regain it, I had to reinstall the app and recover my account - a process that felt oddly unsettling. My Facebook held sentimental value; it was filled with pictures of Enrico and me, capturing moments I thought mattered.

Not long after, I received a message on Facebook Messenger from a Russian woman named Vera Khadeeva. She claimed Enrico had been pursuing her romantically for months. She had seen our pictures and decided to reach out to tell me what he'd really been up to. Intrigued but sceptical, I casually brought up Vera's message to Enrico. His response was to laugh, along with Ross, when he shared it with him, and that reaction spoke volumes. In that moment, I understood more than I let on, and I decided not to dig any deeper.

In her message, Vera explained that she kept leading Enrico on, flirting with him, hoping to recover her unpaid wages. She claimed she had been his lover and a subordinate when he was running GPS - Grouped Property Services.

I replied tersely, advising her to use the proper channels to chase her money. Flirting with former bosses was off-limits and more telling of her character than his.

Some days later, Vera retaliated by sending another round of spiteful messages to my daughter, Shirina Holmatova, through Facebook Messenger. Shirina was just an innocent teenager, clueless about Enrico's issues or romantic misdemeanours. That barbaric gesture - attacking a child after failing to get the desired result, though I wasn't even sure what she had hoped to achieve - concluded it all for me. I rationalised it in my head: Enrico must have dodged a bullet there.

Then there was Kristina.

Kristina was someone Enrico had seriously pined for, a figure who lingered in his thoughts long after their time together. She was Eastern European, strikingly beautiful, with delicate features and mousy brown hair. Fourteen years his junior, she embodied a youthful vitality that both intrigued and intimidated him. Kristina was Enrico's first tentative, almost hesitant step toward exploring the boundaries of his own sexuality - an area long neglected in his marriage to Belinda Pucci.

Belinda, a conservative teacher by profession, had always been steady and predictable. She valued tradition and composure, qualities Enrico admired at first but later felt trapped by. Kristina, on the other hand, represented everything he felt he had missed - passion, spontaneity, freedom. She was a glimpse into a life he had barely dared to imagine, let alone pursue.

Kristina was real in a way that few others had been in Enrico's life. Unlike the hundreds of fleeting pursuits he entertained, she wasn't just another conquest. Their connection had an intensity that stayed with him, so much so that they moved in together for a time.

Enrico recounted memories of her - vivid, detailed - that I believe, even with his most elaborate skills of conmanship, he couldn't have fabricated. These memories were real. Tangible. Filled with passion and undeniable lust. Their time together was intoxicating, but it wasn't just the private moments that haunted him - it was the judgment they faced when they stepped into the world.

They were often mistaken for father and daughter, a sting Enrico never quite shook. The stigma clung to them like a shadow, a constant reminder of how different they looked. He never said it, but I knew he hated those moments - seeing the age in his own reflection contrasted so sharply with Kristina's glow. It wasn't just society's judgment. It was his own.

But Kristina was more than just a young lover. She was a symbol. To Enrico, she was every risk he hadn't taken, every desire he'd buried under practicality and restraint. She was a brief chapter, yes, but one that burned bright enough to leave a mark.

Even as time passed, it was clear - she was etched into his thoughts, a bittersweet reminder of when he dared to defy convention, if only for a moment.

Over time, I pieced together a mental image of Enrico's past - a complex, troubling history of being a "player." Correction: a player with means and resources. Beyond the unsolicited confessions from others, Enrico himself was candid about his past. And somehow, that honesty, paradoxically, became the cornerstone of my emotional security. Despite his history, I felt safe with him - for a little while.

The Rings

In January 2019, Enrico and I spent a week on the Gold Coast. The trip was pre-planned and carried the most romantic purpose. Enrico intended to propose. I was the happiest I had ever been - a mother of two children, privileged enough to be proposed to for the third time. But in the end, the proposal didn't happen. Enrico had the perfect excuse: neither the setting nor the ring, he claimed, was worthy enough for such a moment. I had never felt so special in my life. It was the best holiday on the Gold Coast, and I returned from that trip without a ring.

At first, I was furious. I felt cheated - lured to the Gold Coast under the pretext of a proposal, only to be robbed of the experience. I stormed out of the hotel room to take a walk along the beach. During my walk, Enrico called me several times, asking me to return. I didn't answer. Forty minutes into my walk, having made my way from Surfers Paradise to Broadbeach, I finally picked up. He asked me again to come back, promising I would be pleasantly surprised when I did.

There was indeed a surprise waiting for me when I returned. The ultimate romance on wheels - a premium room service trolley for newly engaged couples - was set in the hallway, impossible to miss.

The experience began with fresh flowers, stunningly arranged, and soft candlelight, setting the perfect stage for an evening of commitment - not engagement. The exquisite selection of gourmet dishes - from tender filet mignon and decadent lobster tail to artisanal desserts and hand-rolled truffles - made every bite a celebration of flavour and sophistication. Fine wines and sparkling champagne completed our meal, elevating it further with a final indulgence: chocolates on a plate bearing the carefully written words "happy engagement."

The first ring came in March 2019 - a classic round-cut, single-stone diamond set in a white gold band. In less than a month, the band showed signs of rust, and a crack appeared on the stone. A jeweller examined the ring, repeatedly asking who had told me it was gold or diamond. I was devastated. But Enrico had a perfect excuse.

The real ring, he explained, was being custom-crafted by jewellers who worked with prestigious brands like Cartier. The Star Jewellers were reportedly sourcing an exquisite 34-carat lab-grown champagne diamond - one of the most luxurious of its kind

- while we discussed the tarnished ring. Enrico and I spent over six months designing the new ring. We patiently waited for the stone to arrive from Colombia. We meticulously reviewed every drawing, colour-matching side diamonds to the centre stone. Enrico proposed to me with the finished ring on February 14, 2020. It was a romantic gesture, a memorable night - except that weeks later, I was served with a legal letter stating that the ring had been stolen from the jeweller's office. Once again, Enrico had all the excuses, explaining what had happened and why the jeweller was in the wrong.

By the time we ventured out for ring number three, all the way to Cherones in Sydney CBD in late December 2020, I had already discovered the drawer in Enrico's Kent Street apartment. Inside, he kept a pouch full of yet-to-be-worn, tarnished fake diamond rings, bulk purchased from Ali-Baba.

I never told him about this discovery. I didn't see the point in talking anymore. I didn't want words. I wanted action. So I waited - quietly, patiently - for the right time.

The Cohabitation

A few weeks into our engagement in January 2019 on the Gold Coast, our conversations began to shift. Wedding planning took a backseat as Enrico's focus turned to the mounting commercial pressures he was facing. These pressures, as he described them, understandably overshadowed any leisurely plans for celebration - financial issues took precedence. Discussions about his struggles became a recurring theme, and I had no reason to doubt the gravity of his situation. I witnessed countless moments where Enrico engaged in tense discussions - both in person and over the phone - with his business clients, trying to recover overdue payments. One particularly dramatic incident stood out, underscoring just how deep the challenges ran.

One of Enrico's largest clients, Criniti's, a well-known chain of upscale restaurants, had defaulted on significant payments. With each partial, so-called goodwill settlement, the outstanding debt kept growing until it reached a level that raised serious concerns - not just about Criniti's solvency but about Enrico's ability to keep his business running. The situation was dire. In the value chain of transactions, the flow of funds within trading terms was essential because many of these payments were ultimately treated as "wages" by the time they reached the workers. Regulatory agencies like Fair Work, the Tax Office, and the State Revenue Office often disregarded how these payments were labeled in contracts, instead judging them by "context." This meant that even if workers were designated as independent contractors, agencies could still deem them "employees" - a classification often referred to in business circles as "deemed employees."

From my conversations with Enrico, I learned that the debt Criniti's owed had exceeded one million dollars. I wasn't privy to the full scale of Enrico's operations, but it was clear that amount was significant. If his business had an annual turnover of $100 million, maybe he could have absorbed the blow. But if it were closer to $10 million, with limited assets beyond receivables, this kind of loss could be catastrophic. Judging by the anxiety and anguish he displayed, I suspected it was the latter - a small operation reliant on strict working capital management, with receivables forming the backbone of its stability. The biggest threat wasn't internal mismanagement of funds; it was clients upstream failing to pay on time.

One event in the spring of 2019 starkly illustrated the severity of his financial predicament. I witnessed him storm into Criniti's flagship restaurant at Darling Harbour, demanding to observe and document every EFTPOS transaction from incoming patrons. He wanted to verify whether Frank Criniti's claims - that the business was struggling and couldn't pay - were even true. The confrontation escalated quickly. Enrico was asked to leave. He refused. Voices rose, and the exchange turned into a heated verbal altercation. At one point, Enrico removed the EFTPOS machine from its cradle and tried to walk away with it. Security stepped in, forcing him to give it back.

As a bystander, I was struck by the intensity of the scene.

Enrico's desperation was palpable, and what I saw made it painfully clear just how deep his financial troubles ran. It was a vivid reminder of the turmoil he was living through.

On the back of these events, we postponed the wedding. By April 2019, Enrico had nowhere to live, nor could he afford a place, and he moved in with me at my residence in Willoughby, NSW. I lived in a two-bedroom apartment. It was tight, trying to accommodate two of my children, my mother - who had come to stay temporarily to help with my young son - and Enrico.

In May 2019, the quest for a new residence began. Enrico was quick to offer a generously alluring solution: we could move into the family-owned investment property on Hickson Road, Walsh Bay, NSW. We visited the area. My mother came along. We had underestimated just how grand the property looked from the outside, perched in one of Sydney's most prestigious locations. The property smiled out at the iconic Sydney Harbour. Nearby residences came with zoned jetties for multimillion-dollar yachts docked alongside. Walsh Bay epitomised refined urban living infused with a serene waterfront charm. It was far beyond what we had hoped for.

We, however, couldn't visit the property. According to Enrico, it was still tenanted. The lease, he explained, had been signed a year or so ago. We needed time to let them vacate.

The question of vacating Walsh Bay became never-ending. Heated conversations followed as I tried to make sense of the reasons he offered week after week. Our living arrangements remained unresolved. I was once again the working horse - the one with a steady job, no debts, a home - supporting my children, my dependent mother, and Enrico, who lived rent-free in my apartment.

More broken explanations emerged - writ of possession, ATO debts, and the property used as collateral by the Australian Tax Office. The conversations were patchy and sporadic. I could never piece them together into anything complete or trustworthy.

Excuses ranged wildly. One night, we physically went to the property. Enrico used a passkey to enter, but the key didn't work. Then, he complained that the real estate agency had changed the code and failed to notify him. He spent time on the phone, seemingly trying to resolve the issue, but the point was - we couldn't get in.

The next excuse: the tenants weren't willing to vacate and had declared they would fight Enrico at NCAT - the New South Wales Civil and Administrative Tribunal - citing squatting rights.

There were many excuses. The last was that Enrico had the property vacated, had the keys sorted, and had the ATO issues resolved. He just wasn't feeling well enough to visit the property with me. I insisted he stay home in Willoughby while I took Shirina to check the property. After some objection, he agreed. But before Shirina and I even reached the car, I got a call from Enrico - he was fitting on the floor. I will elaborate on the fitting business later.

We never made it to Walsh Bay.

By September 2019, I had given up on Walsh Bay. I found a nice place in Neutral Bay, on Wonka Street. An architectural find in its own right, it was a two-story apartment overlooking a playground. The property was a non-traditional, cottage-style, double-story building tucked at the end of a closed-end street. We all visited the property - Shirina, Enrico, Mum, and I, with Kamron, my son, in my arms. We loved it. Enrico looked chuffed. His only problem was that he didn't have a license. He'd lost it to driving offences some time ago. He regularly caught a direct bus from Willoughby to the City, travelling to work and back.

Enrico was in charge of finalising the lease deposit, and I did my part by submitting the application. I received several calls from the property agent, chasing for the deposit. Each time the agent called, I called Enrico, asking what was going on. Speaking with Enrico, one would think the agent was drastically confused. According to him, he'd done everything - just give it a day; the transfer needed time to clear. Then, I stopped getting calls, and one day, I saw the Wonka Street property listed online as leased. It was gone. Enrico never put in the deposit.

We argued. I was deflated, angry, and disappointed. I wanted him to leave and never come back. I was many things. Most importantly, I was helpless.

The last property we tried to move into together was on Sydney Street in Willoughby. Sometime in March 2020, we went to inspect it. We loved it. Except, Enrico never showed up on the day of the move. I called several times. Then I checked his side of the wardrobe in our bedroom and realised he'd cleared out all his things. He had abandoned us.

Shirina had moved out of my Willoughby residence in December 2019 but was planning to move back in with us into the Sydney Street villa. She was left outside, sitting on the kerb with her boxes packed, waiting to be picked up by Enrico - who never showed up that day.

Except, he did show up again two days later.

The Unpaid Debt

The real trouble began after I loaned him $95,000 for eight days. The pretext for the loan was a business-related cash flow issue that affected his ability to pay staff wages. The cash flow crisis was imminent. He needed the money to meet his payroll obligations, which are heavily regulated in Australia.

It happened in mid-2019. The loan was meant to last eight days. Enrico was supposed to get paid by his clients and refund me the money. He only asked for $95,000 AUD. In the grand scheme of things, and with the millions that were often part of our discussions, it seemed like a small amount to loan to someone running a sizable business. Little did I know at the time that, on a net asset basis, I was significantly wealthier than Enrico. Most of Enrico's wealth was built on reckless financing, credit facilities, and a sickening need to keep up with the Joneses just to stay in the game. Enrico had more debts than assets.

I transferred the money; he never acknowledged the receipt in writing. Instead, he called to thank me.

Transfer Between Banks

Eight days came and went. I asked if the repayment was underway. Enrico claimed the transfer had been done. The money, he said, was coming from his Commonwealth Bank (CBA) account and might take up to a week to reach my account at St. George Bank. A week passed. Nothing came.

While having lunch at a local café, I mentioned to Enrico that no money had hit my account. He looked visibly annoyed and assured me he would have a serious word with the bank. Stepping aside, he appeared to make a call, pacing back and forth in what looked like an intense conversation.

When he returned, Enrico explained that the bank had flagged the transfer due to the amount, citing security concerns. He assured me he had spoken to them, clarified that the transaction was legitimate, and convinced them to approve it. According to him, the bank had now given the green light for the transfer to proceed - it was just a matter of waiting. He sounded frustrated, but confident the issue was resolved.

Another week passed. Still nothing. I became increasingly uneasy. At this point, Enrico was blaming the bank entirely, claiming he was having serious relationship issues with them. He began threatening to move his business elsewhere if they continued to "let him down" like this. He acted embarrassed on the bank's behalf, shaking his head as he recounted their supposed incompetence. He regularly told me stories about heated phone calls with bank representatives, casting himself as someone stuck in the middle of a bureaucratic nightmare.

Two more weeks went by. I couldn't take the vague explanations anymore. The back-and-forth with the so-called bank had gotten us nowhere. I demanded he provide me with something in writing - something from the bank - to prove there was a legitimate issue. If there was indeed a delay, I wanted documentation I could take to the proper authorities to resolve it once and for all. Enrico hesitated, brushing me off, saying that banks don't typically issue letters for such scenarios and that he was working on it. I stood firm. I needed proof.

Another week passed. Then another. Still no documentation. My patience had worn thin. It all came to a head during a screaming match at my residence. I was furious, and he seemed rattled by my anger. In the heat of the moment, he finally handed over what he claimed was communication between himself and the bank. Relieved but sceptical, I took the papers and immediately headed to the nearest Commonwealth Bank branch to verify their authenticity.

At the branch, the manager greeted me and carefully examined the supposed bank communication. The first thing we both noticed was how off it looked. The templated message contained glaring spelling errors - something uncommon for any professional correspondence from a financial institution. But the branch manager pointed out an even bigger issue.

"It's not just the spelling errors," he said, his tone suddenly serious. "The problem is the template itself. We don't send out messages like this to clients. This isn't a genuine CBA communication. You need to go to the police."

My stomach dropped. I stood there, frozen, trying to process what I had just heard. A rush of fear and disbelief washed over me. I had suspected for some time that Enrico wasn't telling me the whole truth, but now I was faced with something far worse. I realized, with a sinking heart, that Enrico was not just unreliable - he was a liar.

And the next piece of news hit me like a punch to the gut: Enrico was a con man.

Then, it unfolded step by step.

Depositing Valueless Cheques

Enrico couldn't believe how easy it was to make the Commonwealth Bank look bad. They practically did the work for him. Their incompetence was a goldmine - misleading templates riddled with errors? Perfect. He played the part of the wronged man like a pro, sowing just enough doubt and letting their own mistakes do the rest. Trust a bank like that? Please. Now, he was "moving" everything to ANZ. That was it for him with CBA.

Every good con knows when to switch the stage.

Enrico didn't trust CBA anymore. He also didn't trust the expediency of interbank transfers. So, his new game plan was simple - deposit valueless cheques into my bank account.

Six cheques in total. Each one deposited exactly a week apart. And every single one bounced.

The worst came with the last cheque. Its failure triggered a cascade that froze all of my bank accounts. St. George Bank flagged the activity as suspicious and locked me out entirely. I couldn't pay bills, couldn't access savings, couldn't even swipe my card for groceries. My life ground to a halt, one bounced cheque at a time.

Six weeks passed before St. George finally scheduled an in-person meeting. The branch was located inside the Miranda Westfield shopping centre. Ahead of the meeting, they asked me to bring everything - full 100 points of ID: passport, driver's license, supporting documents. It felt like overkill, but I understood. After what had happened, they needed to verify everything.

Enrico volunteered to come with me. At the time, I almost took it as a kind gesture - him being supportive, him wanting to help. But looking back, I see it differently now. He needed to know what I would find out. What the bank would say. Whether his name would come up, whether he was implicated. The best way to control that narrative was to be right there beside me.

When the day came, I was ushered into a small office within the branch. Two employees sat across from me. They dialed the Banking Security team and put me on the phone. The questions came quickly.

Did I know anything about the cheques that had been deposited weekly?

Did I realize they were all bouncing?

And most importantly - did I know the cheques were issued in the name of Belinda Pucci, Enrico's ex-wife? And that the account tied to them had been closed for years?

I sat there stunned.

I had no idea the cheques were connected to Belinda. I certainly didn't know they were coming from a closed account. The realization hit me like a punch to the gut. While I tried to answer their questions, my mind raced. Why would Belinda send cheques to me?

Or rather, why would Enrico use her name?

Why would he involve me in something so calculated, so deceitful?

Thankfully, at the end of the interview, the bank decided to unlock my accounts. But the relief was brief. It was eclipsed by the weight in my chest on the ride home.

Enrico sat beside me on the train, silent. He didn't need to say anything, and neither did I. We both knew the truth now.

He was a con.

The betrayal cut deeper than I had expected. It wasn't just about the money, or the frozen accounts, or the weeks of financial chaos. It was that he had dragged people close to him - family, friends, even me - into his web, his abyss. It was the fact that he'd used his ex-wife's identity to move money that didn't exist. That he had schemed, lied, and manipulated.

And worst of all, he'd done it while holding my hand. While calling himself my fiancé.

I couldn't stop replaying everything I had learned. And with each passing thought, I kept asking myself the same question:

How much of this relationship was ever even real?

In-Branch Transfer

By then, I was done - done with Enrico's blatant scams, done with the stories that shifted like sand, done with waiting. I needed him to come to the bank with me, to stand there in person, and complete the transfer. No more delays. No more dodging. We both needed to bring a 100-point identification. It should've been simple. But with Enrico, nothing ever was.

As it turned out, he didn't have a driving license. That was the first hurdle. Then, apparently, he didn't have a passport either. Weeks dragged on, with Enrico insisting he was trying to retrieve it from the police. According to him, one of his bail conditions involved a travel restriction, which meant he'd surrendered his passport to the NSW Police. The "state," he said, was prosecuting him for long-standing, serious driving offences.

It sounded plausible - on the surface. But with Enrico, the surface never told the full story. His tales always lived somewhere between truth and fiction, in that murky space where certainty evaporated. What made me even more sceptical was how easily those supposed restrictions vanished whenever we traveled together - to Singapore, to Bali. The barriers that held him back in daily life always seemed to dissolve when leisure was involved.

Weeks passed, full of excuses and full-blown screaming matches. I pushed him out of my apartment one day, physically shoved him, frustration spilling over. And that's when, suddenly, he remembered - he had an Italian passport. Apparently, he could use that for the transfer.

Another twist in his endless narrative, but I was willing to try anything just to end it. We agreed to meet near the Pitt Street branch of ANZ Bank in Sydney, midday.

At the time, I worked for a small maintenance company, mostly from their Central Coast office. To make it work, I arranged to visit their head office on Williams Street, just blocks from the bank. It wasn't convenient, but I was determined. I made the trip to the city, ready to finally sort this out. And to my surprise, Enrico made the trip too. Though now, I wonder if "effort" is even the right word.

We walked together toward the bank. For the briefest moment, I let hope sneak in - maybe this time, we'd finish what we started.

But drama never stayed far behind.

Just seventy meters from the bank, without warning, Enrico collapsed. His body jerked violently, limbs flailing. Full-blown seizures took hold. Foam gathered at the corners of his mouth as he writhed on the pavement, utterly consumed.

A crowd formed fast. Someone yelled that they were a nurse kneeling beside him, checking vitals with calm precision. Others scrambled, calling for an ambulance. Faces lined the circle - strangers offering help, their concern genuine, their empathy pouring out. Strangers, giving everything to someone who would never return the gesture.

And I stood there, frozen. Helpless. Wondering: was this real? Or was this just another act?

After what felt like an eternity, Enrico stirred. He sat up slowly, dazed but conscious. A few men helped him into the taxi I had hailed, and I climbed in beside him. As the taxi pulled away, passing my office on the way, I called in. A "family emergency," I said.

The ride was silent, thick with something I couldn't name. Enrico recovered quickly, brushing it off as if none of it had ever happened. As if we hadn't just lived through chaos. I sat there, sinking, knowing I'd been played - again. I had come to the city, rearranged my day, skipped work, and all of it for nothing. We never made it to the bank. The transfer never happened.

It was just another page in the book of Enrico's excuses.

And then, sometime in 2023, I watched him. I stood beside him at the Italian Embassy in Sydney as he collected an Italian passport. The very document he'd claimed to have, the one he said he'd used three years ago.

He never had it then.

The Judgement

I held the court judgment in my hands through the entire charade Enrico spun, as clear as daylight, as final as anything could be. It was granted on the very first court date - a swift, decisive outcome in my favour. Enrico didn't contest it. He didn't need to. He looked at me, almost smug, and explained that he was perfectly fine with me holding onto it. Why? Because he was certain - absolutely certain - that he'd settle things with me well before I'd ever think about enforcing it.

To him, it was all just a game.

That judgment, firm and valid, sat there growing stale, month after month, as I wasted time - precious time - entertaining Enrico's endless, hollow promises. He had no intention of honouring them. He just kept me tethered long enough in a cycle of hope that I didn't yet know was false.

In Enrico's world, we were still partners. Still bound together, a couple, a team. He reminded me often - too often - that he would repay me, just not now, not all at once, but "in leaps and bounds," as he called it. My expectations, my demands for repayment, made no sense to him. Couples, in his mind, didn't keep score. They merged. They shared. Debts were just another thread in the fabric of their life together. My insistence on separating the finances, on making him accountable - an affront. A betrayal of the dynamic he thought we still had.

And then April 2020 came, and with it, a shift.

I told him I didn't want to be a couple anymore. I didn't want the shared life, the shared debt, the shared lies. I wanted my money. All of it.

Nothing enraged Enrico like the threat of being abandoned. It flipped something inside him, something cold and violent. The man who had once pleaded and feigned helplessness became someone else entirely - someone cruel, someone dangerous. A man who didn't care if he was facing a woman or a man; he would push whoever stood in front of him into a corner, force obedience, demand conformity, all just to hold on.

Enrico requested his lawyer, Derik Carbonara, to file a motion to dismiss my judgment. The grounds? That I had served the claim to the wrong address. The sheer absurdity of it - staggering. Enrico had been living with me in my apartment for years. I had handed him the claim myself. He accepted it without a word. And yet, Carbonara argued that because Enrico's only official ID - issued to replace the ones he'd lost - listed a Melbourne address, my claim was invalid.

The argument was ridiculous. But also frustrating. Because even a ridiculous argument in court can drain you.

If his official address was in Melbourne, how could I have served him legally in Sydney? That was the line they drew.

Carbonara was the kind of lawyer who thrived on this - on red tape and psychological warfare. He reminded me of Roy Cohn, with his ruthless, shameless tactics: never admit, never apologise, never give in. Just wear them down. He didn't seek truth, didn't care for justice. His aim was exhaustion - emotional, mental, and financial.

It worked. It gnawed at me. But it also revealed something else - just how far Enrico would go. Not just to dodge paying what he owed, but to keep his grip on the situation, on me.

Not so different from the Trump and Roy dynamic. Carbonara was the backbone of Enrico's scheme - the one that had fleeced millions from people who never saw their money again.

The Multiple Sclerosis (MS) and Bowel Cancer

Enrico's symptoms began quietly, almost timidly, sometime in early 2019. They crept in, lingered for a while, and then, just as easily, seemed to vanish. But like all things we wish away, they returned - louder this time, more insistent.

I remember sitting through one of his calls to a nurse, my ears straining to catch even the smallest sound from the other end, but hearing nothing but his voice. And yet, I didn't need to hear. The distress on his face told me everything. His eyes were fixed on some distant point as if trying to outrun the words. The results were in - biopsies from seven tumours lining his bowels. Three were cancerous. Bowel cancer, he said, like a sentence passed down by an indifferent jury.

One tumour, the worst, sat near the cusp of his stomach, where it joined the bowel - right at the place where, apparently, the body contracts the most. It was inoperable, he told me, with a finality that left no room for questions.

There were so many emotions spent in those days, maybe not spent - wasted. Wasted in the most devastating way. I remember one night, standing helpless on Coogee Beach, watching him wail like a child beside the manmade kids' pool. His voice broke against the wind, asking the universe, "Why me?" again and again, but the only answer was the sound of the waves.

There were so many tears. One of us cried until the person could cry no more. The other, I think, fed off those tears.

At work, I couldn't escape it. My mobile rang incessantly, and when I didn't answer, the office line would light up. He called relentlessly as if the sound of my voice could ease the aches, the pains he claimed tore through him. My colleagues grew frustrated, but what could I say? There was a lot of helplessness. And more than that, there was fear. Fear of that one word - surgery.

The word "surgery" wasn't just a medical term to Enrico; it was a trigger. A spark that lit every argument. The moment I mentioned it, the air would change. He'd recoil, his eyes wild with something between terror and rage. Surgery was a curse, a voodoo ritual he refused to consider. It didn't matter that the tumours were growing, that they were winning. He wouldn't hear of it.

Looking back, I see it now - the pattern. Every time the tension over the debt rose, his health seemed to deteriorate. It wasn't just cancer. It was multiple sclerosis, too, diagnosed just when things became unbearable. Lesions on his brain, he said. And then the seizures came - violent, shocking, sudden. I can still see him crumpled on the floor, his body convulsing, his face contorted. Strangers rushing to his side, drawn in by the spectacle of suffering. They pulled him back from the brink with their hands, their pity, never knowing.

But beneath all that chaos, something else was taking shape. A truth, quiet and relentless. These episodes weren't just illness. They were something more. They deflected, they distracted. They turned the conversation away from what mattered - from the money he owed, from the promises unkept. His sickness became the shield, the wall of guilt I couldn't scale.

And for a while, it worked.

For a while, I believed.

Enrico's nurse, I was told, was named Belinda. I never met her, despite the times I asked. She was his Cancer Care Nurse, and her name kept coming up, her presence hovering just out of reach. I saw her name flash on his phone often, urgent, private. I had no reason to think she wasn't real. She told him, he told me, that during a fit, the best way to bring him back was with a cool, wet towel on his forehead.

So many times, we reached for that towel. Every time the stress pushed him over, we knew what to do. Sometimes, when it wasn't enough, we poured water over it while it was lodged on Enrico's forehead, trying to keep it cool, trying to keep him here.

We all knew the ritual. My whole family. And we believed it would help.

One day, I was standing at the stove, stirring something - what exactly, I can't even remember now. The sizzle of the pan was the only sound until I noticed Kamron dart into the kitchen. My four-year-old son, who spoke in fragments but moved with a confidence well beyond his years, reached up to the dining table and grabbed a half-filled glass of water. Without a word, without hesitation, he turned and ran back toward the bedroom.

This wasn't like him.

Of all the things he could've snatched in his playful rush, a glass of water wasn't on the list. Something pulled at me - curiosity, maybe instinct - and I followed.

What I saw stopped me cold.

There, on the bedroom floor, Enrico lay motionless. Kamron, small hands trembling, poured the water over his body, the glass tilting carefully, as if he'd done it before or had been told this was what you did. The cool splash met his still form, a ritual learned too young, too early.

There were times, more than I care to count, when Enrico would vanish into the world of outpatient hospitals. He'd leave in the morning and come back late in the afternoon, claiming chemo had drained him. He'd describe in perfect detail the chemical cocktails pumped into his veins - their names, their side effects, the metallic taste they left on his tongue. He would be sick for days, curled up in bed, pale and broken.

But every time I offered to drive him, to pick him up, the details shifted. The timing never quite worked. Our schedules never aligned. It never happened. Yet, the stories - God, the stories - were so vivid, so rich with clinical precision, I sometimes wondered if even he believed them.

What kind of mind can hold onto that many lies? What do you call it when someone crafts falsehoods so elaborate they almost become real? Is it common? Is there a name for this?

Because lying isn't easy. It's a job - one with no time off. Keeping track of every strand, every twist, every face you wore for every story told. Do they feel a thrill watching someone they love - or claim to love - ride the roller coaster they built from scratch? Is it power? A rush of control? Or is it something deeper - a need, desperate and gnawing, for attention, for drama, for proof they matter?

Lying, I've come to learn, is never just about the lie.

It's self-preservation. A way to dodge the shadows of consequence. For some, it's armor - shielding them from truths too painful to admit, even to themselves. For others, it's control, the only way to make sense of a world that feels like it's always slipping. Some lie to be seen. Some lie to stay invisible.

Pathological liars? They live for the act itself. The rush. The game. To them, it's not about truth or fiction - it's about the story. And how they star in it as the hero, the victim, or sometimes, both.

And then there are empaths - the ones who see too much and feel too deeply. The ones like me.

We don't just hear the lie. We hear the pain behind it. The fear. The need. We rationalize. We forgive. We tell ourselves there's a reason, that the story behind the lie matters more than the lie itself. We try to fix it, to hold the pieces together because that's what we do.

But there's a price.

Because in trying to understand, in trying to love through the lie, we lose ourselves. We let the lies pile up, burying us in guilt, in exhaustion, in silence. Until we don't know where our truth ends and theirs begins.

And sometimes, like Kamron, we just know to pour water.

Because somewhere along the lines, someone told us that's how you save them.

The Gaslighting, Abuse and Manipulation

When Kamron was eight, he hit an interesting phase. A stage where he was too smart to understand some concepts yet too young to grasp others.

One day, when I arrived at the local Public School to pick him up, I saw Kamron walking with his classroom teacher, visibly annoyed. It wasn't just a casual escort to the gate - she was heading straight for me. When she reached me, she explained she needed to confirm whether had been truthful about taking a cab home every day, as no one seemed to pick him up from school.

When I turned to Kamron and asked why he told his teacher that, he avoided eye contact, Kamron digging at the soft ground with a long stick. Without looking at either of us, he muttered, "She's lying, she's lying."

Later, after talking further with his teacher and hearing her describe the many behavioural challenges she was facing with Kamron in class, I began piecing together the truth. He had fabricated the story to avoid this very situation - he didn't want her to meet me to complain about his behaviour. Yet, in his mind, he blamed her for doing exactly what he was doing to her: accusing her of lying.

Children often pass through a developmental phase where truth is fluid, almost imaginative. At this tender age, typically between 3 and 7, their understanding of lies versus truth isn't fully formed. It's not rooted in malice or dishonesty; it's simply part of their growing cognitive and moral awareness.

In this phase, children might tell fantastical tales or stretch real events, blending reality with the vivid imagination that defines much of early childhood. They might swear they saw a dragon in the backyard or that they performed heroic feats that never happened. To them, these stories feel real because they reflect what they wish or feel, not a deliberate intent to deceive.

The key for parents isn't just to correct these untruths but to guide them gently - exploring with them the difference between imagination and reality. It's a way of laying the groundwork for understanding why honesty matters and how trust is built without crushing their creative exploration.

Kamron and I would often talk about the difference between truths and fabrications. I'd give him examples, and he'd look up, smug, cute, and so bright. I asked him if he knew the difference, and he said he did.

Two days later, at the dinner table, he declared that I owed him an apology because I had lied - I said we were having chicken for dinner, but it was fish.

We soon found ourselves in a more nuanced discussion about "intentional lies" versus "innocent lies influenced by external factors" and even "lies that feel and appear almost indistinguishable from the truth." What unfolded was the realization that there are countless shades of what we call the same thing. This became especially clear as my astoundingly curious eight-year-old fired off sharp, thought-provoking questions, hungry for answers. And for the first time, I saw that my own understanding of truth and falsehood was shaped by deeply ingrained values. What I knew as true or false was bound tightly with cultural history and personal beliefs - the definition of truth itself was broader, more complex than I'd imagined.

Truth varies and is shaped by a mix of culture, psychology, and experience. Culture is the lens through which we see the world, instilling norms, values, and traditions that shape reality. What's seen as a universal truth by one group might be subjective to another, coloured by deeply rooted social patterns.

Psychologically, our own experiences, biases, and mental frameworks shape what we see. Two people witnessing the same event can walk away with entirely different stories based on emotions, memories, or even subconscious expectations. Language adds more layers - words used to define truth are open to interpretation, tone, and emphasis. What results is a mosaic of perspectives, truth not a fixed point, but something shaped by who we are, how we've lived, and the world that's shaped us. Recognizing this takes humility - and a willingness to question our own assumptions.

Then, the truth got more complicated when Shirina offered her perspective on it.

Shirina, my daughter, challenged me on my parenting during one of our arguments. At 23, an aspiring singer-songwriter, she was living with her boyfriend in Sydney, NSW. She claimed I was extremely hard on her. Some of the things I said as a parent, she told me, left deep marks. She said I was markedly stricter with her growing up, and through her adolescent years, she watched as I let Kamron slide, "almost committing murder and not taking instructions," as she put it. She said she was scarred by the way I raised her.

As we argued, it became clear that our perceptions of her upbringing existed in different worlds. I had been a hard mum, no doubt. I saw a huge potential in Shirina, and I pushed her to reach it. Before singing, she did 14 hours of dance every week at one of the most prestigious dance schools in Sydney. She took drama with a troupe of community performers on the Northern Beaches. She played the flute once a week and was part of the school band. There wasn't a single day in her week that wasn't filled with something - something more, something extra beyond regular school.

I wasn't just there. I was involved. I helped her practice the flute, watched her rehearse dance moves in our living room, giving her feedback on every step. I drove her to every class, every lesson, and sat through nearly a thousand competitions, performances, shows. I loved it - loved watching her progress, each level she reached, each time she turned effort into an art. She was my hard work. My trophy, my creation, my genes.

At the time of our argument, Shirina had over a million followers on TikTok, just short of another million on Instagram. She was travelling the world, getting ready to sign with a record label in LA.

I truly believed I'd taken her as far as I could with the resources I had.

She truly believed I had been too hard.

There we stood - two people with two different yet undeniable truths. Her truth was shaped by the moments she remembered, by the years when all she could see was a mother pushing, chastising, pushing again. My truth stretched far beyond her childhood - through years before she was born, through commitments, sacrifices, and compromises she could never see. I remembered sleepless nights, like the time she burned with fever in my arms, barely ten years old. By morning, she was running again, off to school, while I dragged myself through a full workday, running on fumes.

I remembered getting the news that my grandmother had passed - the person I loved most. But I didn't fly to her funeral. I couldn't. As a single mother, I couldn't leave Shirina or disrupt her schooling. I stayed. I remembered saving every cent I could to pay for her braces, making sure they came off after two years. All the small things I denied myself so she could keep moving forward.

I even left everything behind and moved us to Australia, determined to give her what I never had - opportunities and a future. I gave up my career and my life as I knew it.

And yet, I couldn't deny her truth.

Her reality had been shaped by her own DNA, intertwined now with new cultural norms and societal expectations. Her truth was as valid as mine, no matter how much it clashed with what I believed.

Truth looked even more different if I thought about my nephews.

I am from the tail end of the USSR generation. The collapse meant I was given money to take to school that looked nothing like the old Soviet rubles. These were Uzbek soums, my parents told me. As inflation soared, the number of soums I had to bring went from a few notes to wads of cash just to buy lunch in the school canteen. Prices changed daily until no one could keep up. I learned that the price of the same cookie had gone up by another few million soums at the very moment I tried to buy it.

Food vanished from the shelves. Supermarket doors had queues hours before they opened. Rationing started - a family of four was allowed one loaf of bread per day. Chaos reigned. I was just a teenager trying to graduate, trying to make sense of it all, mostly oblivious to how much the world around me had changed.

A whole new truth hit me not long after. It was the summer of 1994. My father told me I was going to apply to the "National (Uzbek)" cohort for university. I was furious. I'd spent ten years studying in the "European (Russian)" stream - I barely spoke Uzbek. I ranted, I raved, I threw every argument I could. I told him there was no way I could pass an Uzbek-language entry exam. It felt like he was placing an impossible weight on me, pushing me into something I wasn't ready for, didn't want.

But my father stayed firm. The political atmosphere in Uzbekistan was changing, he said. Russian-speaking graduates had no future there. Not anymore.

University entry was brutal. The top 10% got in for free, with a monthly stipend. The next 90% had to have a sponsor - usually an employer. The rest? They dropped out before they could even start.

After weeks of cramming, of being tutored, of trying to wrap my head around Uzbek academic jargon, I scraped in. Barely. My name was the last on the list, right above the cut-off for stipend-funded entrants.

Once I got in, the world I knew slipped away. My curriculum felt stripped down and less challenging. Political subjects crept in, preaching the greatness of our current government. The whole environment was deeply anti-Russian, a relentless push to reclaim an Uzbek identity - one we were told had been stolen during the Soviet years. I stood out. Everything about me reeked of Russian education, and they saw it.

One day, walking to class, a group of guys from my cohort shouted at me. "Silver platter metropolitan girl." It wasn't the first time. I'd been called worse. Urban, soulless, science-obsessed. Someone who had lost her culture and sold her identity to the Europeans.

But that day, I didn't walk away. I walked straight up to them. They were crouched on the ground, laughing, sure I wouldn't say a word. I asked them - what exactly was their problem with me being raised in a European environment?

One of them stood up. His father worked the farms, he said, to pay for families like mine to play "important" in the hands Soviet invaders. He said I didn't know hardship, didn't even know how to do the basics - like milking a cow.

"I know how to milk a cow," I shot back.

"How?" he asked.

"You put a bucket under the cow, right where the tits are. You pat it, signal you're about to milk it, then with smooth, confident strides, you milk the cow - across all eight tits."

Eight-tit-cow. That was my nickname for two whole terms. For those desperately trying to fit in like I did, here's something useful: cows only have four tits.

Then came the nickname number two - Naked-truth. In Uzbek, "naked" doesn't mean bare, stripped down to honesty - it means physically naked. The closest they had to what I meant was "bitter truth." It happened in philosophy class. I was presenting in Uzbek, explaining a concept, and two minutes in, the whole cohort was in stitches.

Still, I made it. I finished that first year, stumbling through a language that was mine but wasn't, trying to hold my ground while learning it all over again.

During the summer holidays, I went to visit my uncle and my nephews. They told me they were studying in Uzbek too - but not my Uzbek. Not the kind written in Cyrillic. Their Uzbek was written in the Latin alphabet, closer to Turkish. It wasn't just language. Everything had changed. The government. The ideology. What it meant to be Russian, what it meant to be Uzbek. The alphabet, the textbooks, the very history we were taught - it was all rewritten.

My nephews had their truth, too. They believed, without question, that Uzbekistan had been invaded by the Red Army and that it was forced into the USSR. Their truth ran deep, and it clashed with everything I'd ever known. I was raised on stories of scattered Mongol, Turkish, and Persian empires, fighting among themselves, finding peace only under the Soviet banner, calling it Uzbekistan.

The concept of truth with Enrico took on the shape of dark matter - something without beginning or end, something that shifted, expanded, consumed, and never let go.

I was gaslighted in ways I couldn't even name at the time. Medical issues aside, Enrico always had a way of dragging me back in, using extremes to make me question the very idea of leaving.

There was one time, in the winter of 2020, when he lived in the Lumiere apartment block on Bathurst Street, right in the heart of

Sydney's CBD. I remember the day clearly - I was wearing my favourite lambskin brown leather jacket, heading out to meet a digital marketing group I'd joined, mostly for LinkedIn networking. We had argued, again. It always circled back to the same thing - the debt he owed me, and his endless excuses.

But that night, the argument didn't just escalate. It exploded.

Suddenly, Enrico climbed onto the window frame, one leg in, one leg out, his torso twisted awkwardly, suspended in the middle. It was the only window in the bedroom of his high-rise apartment, and the dizzying drop outside was real. I stood frozen, watching him teeter between life and death. My heart pounded in my throat as I begged him to stop, to get down, to not do this.

I was paralysed, trapped in the shock of what he was willing to do. The sheer audacity of it, the recklessness - it hit me like a wave, pulling me under. I couldn't breathe. Couldn't think. The fear, the confusion, the guilt - it all collided in that tiny room, suffocating me. Time stopped. I couldn't understand how we had gotten here. How a fight about money had become a threat against life itself. He balanced there, between the glass and the air, and I knew then that this was no longer about debt. It was about control. About fear.

And it wasn't the only time.

There was the day he almost threw himself into traffic, into a blur of cars flying past at 70 kilometres an hour. I grabbed him. I used every ounce of strength I had - small, shaking arms trying to pull back a man twice my size. I don't even remember how I did it. Only that when it was over, I had nothing left. No breath. No strength. No clarity to end it, to walk away like I should have.

And then there was the garage.

He spiralled again, this time from panic into something deeper, darker - shock, maybe, or something beyond it. I watched, unable to move, as he picked up a commercial-grade extension cord, looped it over the steel beam that supported the roof of his father's garage, and tied the other end around his neck. He stepped onto a chair, adjusting the cord, preparing.

For a few seconds, I didn't know what to do. My hands fumbled for my phone. I started filming. I stopped. I tried talking to him, reasoning, begging. I dialled an ambulance. I hung up. It all blurred together - seconds stretched into lifetimes. The video, short as it was, caught everything. Him getting caught, stuck, as the cord tightened around his neck. His voice cracking, screaming, "I'm stuck, I'm stuck."

That image haunts me. The sound, more.

And after everything, after all of it, I still believed I was special. Like every other woman before me, I clung to the thought that I was different. Because he almost died to be with me.

I can still hear him, the desperation in his voice - "I'm stuck, I'm stuck."

It took me days to recover from manoeuvres like that. Days to piece myself back together, to push the image of him dangling there, caught in his own madness, to the back of my mind. But just like the others he'd gaslighted before me, I thought I was the exception. The one who mattered more. The one he couldn't live without. After all, hadn't he almost killed himself to stay in my life?

But gaslighting wasn't his only weapon.

Enrico had his limits. And when he reached them - when he felt truly threatened, when I showed even the slightest gesture of leaving - he changed. The fear of abandonment twisted him into something else entirely. Something darker. A monster with no hesitation.

He had crafted this persona, a carefully constructed façade of power and connection. He often spoke of his ties to the underworld, of men who owed him favours. Not the kind you ask for in daylight and not the kind anyone would ever admit to. These weren't just associates; they were people, he said, who handled things. People you wouldn't want to cross.

I remember the way he spoke of his mother's funeral, how the streets had filled with mourners - four hundred, he claimed - stretching the entire length of the block. Like a cult, they came not just to grieve but to honour. Many of them hadn't even known her, but they knew the family. And that was enough.

He painted it like a scene from another world: a line of handcrafted black cars, each one more extravagant than the last, moving slowly behind a funeral car so lavish it seemed unreal, draped in a waterfall of flowers. The whole thing a grand, solemn show - a testament, not just to loss, but to legacy.

Years later, in October 2024, I stumbled upon an article in the *Daily Mail* about the funeral of a prominent figure in the Bandidos chapter on the mid-North Coast of NSW. The piece struck me - it wasn't just a funeral, it was a spectacle. A ceremony heavy with symbolism, steeped in a kind of reverence that only certain circles could understand. It was a statement, a final act of honour within a world where loyalty and reputation were everything.

And I couldn't help but think of Enrico, of the way he had described his mother's funeral with the same kind of grandeur, the same sense of belonging to something larger, something formidable. But now, looking back, I saw it for what it was - a story. A fabrication. His connection to that world was nothing more than an idea he sold, a narrative he crafted. The network he claimed so fiercely - it didn't exist. And soon, I would learn that for myself.

One of our arguments, like so many before, spiralled. Words, sharp and relentless, ricocheted between us until I was done - tired, depleted, beyond compromise. I told him to leave. I needed him out of my apartment, out of my life. But Enrico didn't leave. He never left when I asked.

I turned, heading towards my neighbour's apartment on the upper floor, desperate to put space between us, when I felt it - a hand clamping down on my left bicep, hard and unrelenting. The grip was brutal, filled with intent. Before I could react, he spun me around and dragged me, step by step, back down the stairs. I fought him, grabbing at the handrail, but it didn't matter. His strength overwhelmed mine.

Back inside my apartment, he shoved me forward, his hand pressing into my shoulder blade like a brand, marking the boundary I wasn't allowed to cross.

And then came the lecture - the slow, deliberate unspooling of threats disguised as warnings. He spoke again of his "network," of the people he knew who could make things happen, make things disappear. People who wouldn't think twice about stepping in if I ever dared to walk away.

It would be in my best interest, he said, to stay. To keep things as they were. Because the consequences of leaving? They would be far worse than anything I had imagined.

Enrico's 46th Birthday Party

Not capturing the birthday of the century would have been a cardinal sin. By January 2022, I was deep in a string of proposals on the Airtasker app, combing through portfolios with a fine-tooth comb. I wasn't just after any photographer - I needed someone who could capture a specific kind of magic.

Capturing people in motion, the kind of raw, unrehearsed emotion that only candid action photography can deliver, is an art. One that requires not only technical mastery but a sharp, almost instinctive sense of timing. Observation was everything. The power to see, to anticipate, and to freeze those fleeting seconds that slip by unnoticed - that was what I needed. It's this approach that breathes life into photographs, turning moments into something permanent, something that vibrates with energy long after the shutter clicks.

Mastering motion meant understanding how to wield fast shutter speeds to halt time or slow ones to blur it just enough to suggest movement, urgency, and life. Just as crucial was the photographer's ability to fade into the background, to become invisible. Only then would people act naturally, giving you images that didn't feel posed or planned but honest. The kind of shots that, when viewed later, could transport you right back to the pulse of the night - the laughter, the dancing, the connection.

How do I know all this? Because during COVID-19, after losing my job in April 2020, I didn't sit still. I took a short photography course. Macro photography, to be exact. A different beast entirely from action shots but demanding in its own right. Macro took me into another world - the world of detail so small, so intricate, it lived beyond the reach of the naked eye.

Macro photography is a meticulous craft. It's not just about pointing and shooting; it's about understanding your tools - macro lenses, extension tubes, focus stackers - and about patience. The tiniest nudge could shift the entire composition. You work with razor-thin depth of field, constantly adjusting light and experimenting with magnification. It's technical, yes, but deeply creative. I learned to see the universe in the veins of a leaf, in the patterned wing of a butterfly.

Courses in macro photography weren't easy. They taught optics, lighting, and the precision needed to capture something barely there. And yet, it was exactly what I craved. I've always sensed detail before seeing it - before watching it bloom, 400 times magnified, in the lens of my camera.

And now, I truly believe this: the real story is always in the details, in the things that exist just beyond what we think we see.

Like me getting a detailed fine for a vehicle I didn't even know I owned. It arrived in May 2022, like an unwelcome guest at my door. A letter, plain and official, stating I owed money for a car I'd never driven. Confused, I called RMS, hoping for a simple clerical error, but instead, I was told there were more fines coming. This wasn't a mistake.

I called Ross Pucci next, desperate to stop the bleeding. Someone was driving that vehicle, someone I didn't know, and they were racking up fines in my name. I told him whoever it was needed to stop - immediately. But Ross didn't want to talk solutions. We ended up in a screaming match, loud and raw. His voice, accusing. Mine, incredulous.

Ross wasn't concerned about the fines. He wanted to know how many vehicles Enrico had secretly transferred to me. I wanted to know who the hell was driving the only one I'd just learned about. The accusations flew fast. He accused me of collusion, of being part of some grand scheme with Enrico - "husband and wife fleecing the Pucci family." He ranted about secret deals, about Enrico ripping off their business, selling out to third parties behind their backs. I listened, stunned, until I couldn't anymore. I hung up.

The texts came next. Accusations, half-truths, and spite thinly veiled as concern. And then, silence. Gradually, it all faded. But not before I took it to the police, every word logged into my statement, forming the backbone of the sealed ADVO granted a year later.

By June 2022, I had transferred the vehicle. It was no longer my problem. It went to Enrico's father, Alfredo Pucci. I wanted nothing to do with it. There's no joy in owning a luxury car you've never driven, one that bleeds you dry in merit points and fines. It was a burden disguised as status.

Why didn't I go straight to Enrico to resolve it? Why not confront the man who had handed me this mess? It's a fair question. But stay with me - I had my reasons, and they were compelling.

Meanwhile, the photographer did an amazing job. Over 200 images, delivered in RAW format just a week after Enrico's birthday. Every moment captured, every laugh, every glance. And like everything else - paid for by me. This was my project, after all.

Narghiza Ergashova and Enrico Pucci, 2022 – Sydney, Australia. Images from Enrico's 46th Birthday

Final Cohabitation Attempt

"I can stop the rocket with nuclear missiles from launching, but I cannot stop the sinkhole from collapsing." Someone said that in a TV show playing on my screen. I wasn't really watching; my body was there, but my mind was miles away. Still, those words found me, as if I had been waiting for them all along. When I came back, I caught myself mentally repeating them, again and again.

The irony struck me - the sharp contrast between absolute control and complete helplessness, wrapped up in a single line. On one hand, the character claims the power to stop the launch of a nuclear missile - something monumental, complex, a global threat wrapped in wires, codes, and countdowns. On the other, they confess they can't prevent a sinkhole from collapsing - something local, natural, unyielding. A quiet disaster.

This, I realized, is the paradox of human influence. We push the limits of science and technology. We build AI to think for us, satellites to watch over us, and medicines to save us. We seed the clouds with silver iodide, coaxing the sky to rain when we want it to. But once it rains, we can't stop it. Once nature decides, we are just the same small as we were.

We have driverless cars, drones soaring over cities, and yet we can't fix Polycystic Ovary Syndrome - PCOS - a condition that quietly reshapes the lives of up to 13% of women. That's nearly 3.9 billion people affected, waiting for an answer that still doesn't exist.

The balance between what we control and what controls us is fragile. And sometimes, it's not about nature. Sometimes, it's about the people we let in.

I saw myself in that paradox, caught between the illusion of power and the reality of helplessness. The resonance between that line on the screen and what happened between the 6th of October 2020 and the 7th of December 2020 was immediate, visceral.

There were things I thought I controlled. But I didn't.

In the early hours of the 6th of October - 3:48 am, to be exact - while I slept next to him, Enrico was sexting another woman. Her name was Dina Aslan, a lover he'd picked up on RSVP back in May. She was Jordanian, chasing permanent residency in Australia. They weren't shy in their longing. "I wish you were in my arms," Enrico wrote.

And I was right there, breathing beside him, dreaming of a life I thought we were rebuilding.

I'd spent days packing. I was moving into his place - Kent Street, Millers Point. Number 168. A luxury apartment in a gothic building that looked like something out of 1920s New York. Elegant, intimidating. The kind of place where the concierge didn't need white gloves to look polished - they already did.

Just days earlier, Enrico had stood at my door, begging for reconciliation. Move in, marry me, he said. Emails followed, promises scrawled in digital ink - this time, he meant it. This time was different, unlike the hundred times before.

And I? I was vulnerable. I'd lost my job in April, another casualty of COVID-19. I was adrift, with two people depending on me: my son, my mother. The money was running out, and I was tired. So tired. I was at my lowest.

We had just come through our longest, most serious separation, marked by those jagged stops and starts. And I, foolishly, believed. I believed that he finally understood what he stood to lose. I believed that this would break the pattern.

I believed I had control.

The night before the final move, we argued. Again. I told him to delete every picture of me, of us, from his phone. He didn't want to, but he did. His apartment was chaos - expandable plastic bags filled with my things sprawled across the floor, overflowing with clothes, kitchen utensils, the entire medicine cabinet, and Kamron's toys. Nothing was sorted. The furniture was next, but the mess could wait.

Enrico got up at six and made me breakfast, like he always did. The scent of eggs and toast filled the room, but it didn't feel warm. He moved around the kitchen with tight, controlled energy, each motion precise, almost brittle. His jaw was clenched, his eyes hard. The tension sat between us, thick and heavy, like a storm cloud neither of us dared acknowledge.

He didn't say much, and neither did I. We ate in silence, the kind of silence that wasn't peaceful, but loaded - crowded with everything we weren't saying.

I thought about the night before. About how, just hours ago, he was likely still sexting Dina. About how even that didn't seem to scratch the surface. It was never just about the sexual distractions. There was something deeper, something raw and festering beneath the surface. He couldn't let go, not of control, not of power, not of me. And now, as I watched him set down the plate in front of me, I knew he was slipping again - clinging to the smallest ways he could still make me feel small.

We spoke only about the move. The truck. The elevator. He said the building had reserved the lift for us, that he was dealing with the trucking company himself. His words were clipped, mechanical, like he'd rehearsed them to keep from unraveling. I nodded. There was no point pushing. We both knew what was under the surface.

The hours stretched on. We circled around each other, careful, like we were walking a minefield, afraid of setting off something we couldn't put back together.

And then, at 7:45 AM, it detonated.

A message flashed on my phone.

He cancelled the truck. Cancelled the lift.

"You can thank George for this," he wrote.

Enrico's 46ᵗʰ Birthday Party

I had been picturing the perfect cake in my mind for days - a vision so vivid I could almost taste it, yet somehow, it remained just out of reach. I scoured the internet, combing through endless images, but nothing matched what I saw so clearly in my head. Each cake I found felt flat, uninspired, missing the spark, the soul, the personality I was after. Frustration crept in, but I wasn't ready to give up. I turned to Instagram, scrolling through an endless parade of celebrations captured in photos, cakes front and centre. And then, I saw it.

It wasn't perfect, not by any measure, but it had something - an edge, a hint of boldness that made me pause. It was a beginning.

Curious, I tapped on the image and found myself lost in the baker's gallery. I scrolled through her work, frame by frame, studying the details. Her designs weren't polished to perfection, but they breathed creativity. They had life. The more I looked, the more I felt it - our visions aligned. She knew contrast; she understood detail. Her colour choices were brave, her textures daring. There was something about her style that spoke to me. She wasn't just a baker - she was an artist. My kind of artist.

I reached out immediately, sending her a message. And another. She didn't respond at first, leaving me hanging in that unbearable limbo of hope and doubt. But when she finally replied, we exchanged numbers, and I wasted no time. I called her.

Her voice on the other end was exactly what I had hoped for - warm, open, curious. She listened, really listened, as I shared my vision. She was the kind of person who could take someone else's idea and make it her own, blending inspiration with instinct. I could tell from the way she spoke about her craft; this was someone who loved what she did, someone who would treat my cake as more than just another order.

We talked about everything - the colours, the mood, the feel I wanted. Rich gold, burnt orange, deep copper. Bold, but not loud. Elegant, but full of life. Each tier had to hold its own, yet together they needed to tell a story. We talked flavours - layers of sponge, each one chosen to complement not just the look but the essence of the cake. And then there were the words. I needed a custom message, a font that was clean yet striking, something that would tie it all together like a signature.

By the time we hung up, I knew I had found her. This wasn't just going to be a cake. It was going to be a centrepiece. A creation. Something imagined, and now, finally, something real.

When it arrived, I was breathless. It was everything I had hoped for, and more.

The cake stood tall, proud, an extension of the very heart of the celebration. It didn't just sit in the room - it owned it. Behind it, a golden curtain draped softly over its frame, creating a perfect backdrop for photographs. A cascade of balloons in shades of white, brown, orange, and vibrant gold framed the scene, giving it a richness, a warmth that made everyone pause. It was more than decoration - it was art. Every detail had been seen, considered, and perfected. And as the guests gathered, eyes wide with admiration, I knew I had done it.

Enrico's birthday felt like a masterfully directed production, a seamless blend of entertainment and elegance. It was an experience curated with precision - a value chain of carefully chosen elements, each contributing its own charm to the celebration.

From the spectacular cake to the vibrant costumes worn by the dancers, every facet had been meticulously planned. The costumes added a playful flair, nudging guests to shed their inhibitions and step into the festivities. And when the dance lessons began, the room shifted. Everyone came together on the floor, laughter echoing, movements free and unrestrained, creating moments that felt almost electric in their joy. It was as if the entire event had been designed to ignite something deeper, to send every guest's senses - and their hormones - into a frenzy.

There was something almost biological about it, the way each element seemed tailored to stir the chemistry of the brain. Dopamine - the "feel-good" hormone - coursed through us all, released in waves as anticipation turned into exhilaration, and fleeting moments of pleasure crystallized into memories. And then, in quieter pauses, when the music softened and guests mingled, another shift occurred. Serotonin took its place, lifting moods, calming nerves, filling the spaces between conversation with an ease that made strangers feel like old friends.

Why was it so important to me that Enrico had the best birthday he never deserved? Why did I throw myself into it so completely, spending more than I should, ensuring he had everything he could never give back?

Because it was his last birthday outside the cold walls of a corrective facility. He didn't know it yet.

But I did.

I had planned it for months.

The Plan: After the Final Cohabitation Attempt Fails

How far would one go to survive? How deep does self-preservation run in our veins? Survival, for me, quickly distilled into a series of simple equations: heat equals life, food equals strength, complacency equals death.

On the 6th of October 2020, at precisely 7:45 AM, Enrico sent me a message that felt like the final blow. He had cancelled the truck and the reservation for the lift. His words, laced with venom, ended with, "You can thank George for this."

For months, I had been fighting to end things with him, each attempt more draining than the last. He clung on, refusing to release his hold, no matter how clearly I tried to sever ties. A few weeks before that morning, I had taken what I believed to be the definitive step: I blocked him everywhere. Social media, messages, calls - gone. For the first time in three years, there was silence. A fragile peace settled over me, unfamiliar but intoxicating. It was like breathing air that no longer belonged to him.

And with that small, precious space, I dared to hope. I signed up for Tinder - not to fall in love, not to jump into something new, but to remind myself what the world looked like without him. I wanted to see what normal felt like again. Soon enough, I found myself on my first date in what felt like a lifetime. His name was George. He was calm, soft-spoken, present. A stark contrast to the chaos I had been used to. We agreed to meet for coffee at Gloria Jean's in Chatswood. I was nervous, but there was also a flicker of excitement, the possibility of rediscovering who I was without Enrico's shadow looming over me.

The date started gently. We exchanged small talk, eased into laughter, and for a moment, the world felt ordinary again. Until it didn't.

Enrico walked into the café.

Not alone.

By his side was an oversized Middle Eastern woman - taller than him, broader and grander than his commanding presence. She seemed oblivious to the tension that cracked through the air the moment he saw me. To her, it was just another casual outing, but for me, it was a collision course with a past I wasn't ready to face.

Enrico's eyes locked onto mine, and a chill crept through me. I knew that look. I knew what came next.

I leaned toward George, my voice low, urgent. "We need to leave. Now."

He looked confused, but I didn't wait. "My ex-fiancé just walked in."

Without hesitation, we rose, grabbed our things, and walked out. My pulse hammered in my ears as we left the café behind, my mind reeling. Relief battled with dread - relief that I had escaped the immediate fallout, dread knowing that Enrico wouldn't let it go.

Not now.

Not ever.

That evening, hours later, a loud, relentless banging shattered the fragile quiet of my apartment. My stomach turned in on itself. I didn't need to ask who it was. Enrico. His voice, thick with rage, sliced through the door, demanding, pleading, threatening all at once.

"Open the door! Let me in!" he shouted, his fists pounding like thunder against the frame. "You went on a date! After everything I've done for you, I left everything for you!"

Each word was laced with accusation, not just of betrayal, but of possession. To him, I wasn't a person. I was property. His property. And now I had broken some sacred, unspoken rule. I had stepped out of line.

I tried to reason with him, to hold the storm at bay. I reminded him we were separated, that he had been on a date too. That we were free to live our lives.

His voice rose, sharp and indignant. "I was there out of spite! I didn't want her. She's got visa issues - her ex left her stranded. I hate her accent."

Even now, I still don't know if it was a coincidence or a meticulously orchestrated hijack of my date. But one thing I do know - George vanished. Enrico made sure of that. He promised me George would disappear.

And he did.

But Dina Aslan - the Middle Eastern woman - she didn't disappear. Not for years. She lingered, a shadow that flickered in and out of our story, refusing to fade.

The truth about who disappears and who doesn't, who lets go and who holds on with bloodied knuckles, it's not chance. It's psyche. It's the twisted terrain of human attachment we'll come back to later in this story.

In the days that followed, Enrico's rage transformed into something softer, or so it seemed. Desperation wore many masks. Email after email, text after text, phone calls that bled into each other, all carrying the same refrain: Come back. Let's try again. Please.

"Things will be different. I'll fix this. You'll never move on - I won't let you."

He wept. He performed repentance. He begged my mother, pulled on her heartstrings like a virtuoso of guilt. He took Kamron to McDonald's, filled him with sugar and soft promises, whispering the word "family" until it sounded like a lullaby.

And I caved.

Not for love. Not even for hope. For survival.

I told myself he could repay me, if not with money, then with help. We needed to move. I couldn't keep the Willoughby apartment any longer. The bills had risen like floodwaters, and I was drowning. Unemployed, with a son to feed and a mother to care for, I needed something - anything - to lift the weight.

Maybe if he helped, if he carried us through this one moment, something would shift. Maybe this would be the first step back to something we could call normal.

But at 7:45 AM, on the morning we were meant to move, Enrico sent a message.

He'd cancelled everything.

The truck. The lift.

"You can thank George for this," he wrote.

And just like that, everything collapsed again.

To understand Enrico's behaviour, we have to step into the shadowed corridors of possessiveness - the kind that is born from deep insecurity. Possessiveness, at its core, is not about love, but about fear. It's about measuring the worth of a partner not through connection or care, but through how desirable they are to others. And more crucially, how hard they are willing to fight to stay.

Desirability, in this view, is a distorted mirror. It reflects not just beauty or charisma but the struggle - the push and pull that defines whether someone is worth keeping. The insecure mind sees value not in peace, but in proof. Proof that the other is willing to battle for them, to resist leaving, no matter the cost.

This possessiveness plays out in two stark, explicit ways:

1. **Benefit-inducing behaviours.** These are the gestures, the gifts, and the moments of affection meant to make us believe that being with them is a privilege and that leaving would mean forfeiting something valuable.
2. **Cost-inflicting behaviours.** These are the threats, the punishments, the cold calculations meant to make leaving feel like stepping into a storm - where pain is certain, and escape comes at too high a price.

When one partner has drifted away - after months, even years, of being unseen or unheard - the complacent partner often experiences a jolt. A wake-up call. Sometimes, it's subtle, a flicker of fear. Other times, it's a full-blown reckoning. But almost always, it comes too late.

By the time the dormant partner stirs, the bond has frayed beyond repair. The chance to woo back with kindness or understanding has passed. There's no room left for soft, benefit-inducing acts. The shift is sudden and brutal - into cost-inflicting survival mode.

It's not about love anymore. It's about control. About making sure that if they can't have you, no one will. It's a desperate attempt to rewrite the story, to punish the other for leaving. To make them hurt. To reclaim power, even if only through suffering.

"If I can't make you stay, I'll make you regret going."

These actions - manipulations, threats, financial sabotage - are not just cruel; they are futile. They don't rebuild what's been lost. They only deepen the divide, carving out scars where healing might have been possible long ago.

It's a tragic pattern, common but devastating, in relationships where too much has been left unsaid too long. Where neglect festers into resentment, and love turns into war.

And more often than not, this is where the courts come in.

Family law disputes are born from this very dynamic - instigated by the partner who slept through the relationship until the moment they realized it was over. Then, they strike, not to win back affection, but to inflict one last wound.

The one who has already left, in heart if not yet in law, is dragged back into the mess. Not because they care, but because they must defend themselves. Thousands of dollars vanish in legal battles, not for justice, but to soothe a bruised ego. Until, at last, the aggrieved party surrenders - not to love, not to reconciliation, but to reality.

And reality, in the end, does not bargain.

And then, circling back to that morning - October 6th, 2020.

I left everything behind. All of my belongings, the pieces of my life carefully packed and ready for a fresh start, were trapped in Enrico's apartment. My own home stood hollow, stripped bare, its empty shell echoing the loss I hadn't yet fully absorbed. Furniture stood like forgotten sentinels, each wrapped in layers of plastic and bubble wrap, poised for a journey that never began. There were wind corridors weaving through the silence, carrying whispers that felt too much like grief - an eerie melody of what it meant to hit rock bottom.

Instinctively, I reached for the kitchen cupboard, looking for hand sanitizer, something small, something routine after moving heavy things. Instead, I was met with an absence that felt like a slap. Every last item I needed - every tool of survival - was locked away. In his apartment. Held hostage.

I had no laptop, no tablet - no way to apply for jobs, no way to rebuild myself. Just my phone. Four devices left behind, along with the rest of my life. I sent message after message, begging Enrico to return my things. They bounced. He had blocked me.

Shirina tried next. She messaged him, hoping he'd at least listen to her. But he didn't. He sent her abuse, then blocked her too.

Desperate, I called my real estate agent, pleading to extend my tenancy despite having already submitted my notice. Her response was blunt, stripped of compassion: without employment, there was nothing she could do.

I scrambled, clawing at every possibility for a roof over our heads. I needed somewhere - anywhere - for my son to sleep that night, just to get through until morning. A room, a safe corner to gather myself and face the next blow. I found something. Not much, just one bedroom in a house shared with strangers. But it was enough. I secured a storage unit at Kennards, cramming what I could afford into it before maxing out my card. The rest - the pieces I couldn't pay to keep - were left on the curb.

My memories, my history, my life abandoned for the council to erase.

Kamron slept on a bed in that small Airbnb room. I curled up on the floor beside him. My mother - she slept in my car.

But there was one tiny victory in all of this. Just one. Enrico had left me. Not the other way around. He broke it off. He walked away. That meant he wouldn't come back, wouldn't accuse, wouldn't chase me down, dragging me into the same vicious cycle. For the first time, I didn't have to fight him off. He had given up.

And so I told myself, as I lay on that floor, tears soaking into the carpet: this is your ticket out. It hurts. It's brutal. But this is your way out. Hold on.

A lot happened between October 6th and December 7th, 2020.

On October 9th - my birthday - I spent the day at the Chatswood Police Station. There's something surreal about celebrating another year of life while trying to reclaim the fragments of it from someone who refuses to let go. The officers, well-meaning but powerless, watched as Enrico played his familiar games. He told them he was interstate, no idea when he'd return. "What's the rush?" he asked, as if my desperation to retrieve my own belongings was an overreaction.

He insisted we were still together, as though that erased everything, as though being in a relationship gave him the right to strip me of control. Later, an officer emailed me photos of my property, tucked away neatly in different drawers in Enrico's apartment. Along with the images came a copy of Enrico's email: my things were safe, he claimed. All I needed to do was come "home" to collect them.

Two weeks passed before he unblocked me. Then came the calls - sporadic, like ripples on water, unsettling but familiar. Most of what we spoke about revolved around my property. That's all I wanted - just to get back what was mine.

Toward the end of October, we met for breakfast. I needed my laptop - needed it to claw back some sense of normalcy, to work, to live. He said he'd give it to me. He didn't.

Over breakfast, he dropped the next blow. He hadn't brought the laptop. If I wanted it, I'd have to go back to his apartment. And when I did, standing in the doorway of the life I had almost escaped, he laid down the final rule:

"The laptop doesn't leave. You can use it here, but it stays with me."

It was never about the laptop. It never was.

It was hard to maintain a facade of indifference, pretending I was unaffected while dying inside from the weight of it all. Every moment felt like a battle not to crumble. There was no balance in my life; nothing even close. My thoughts ran in circles, my emotions hovered on the brink of collapse. And hardest of all was watching Enrico relish in every moment of manically tearing me down, the cruel smirk on his face like a signature - permanent, deliberate. The words he used, how he dragged them out, how he paused just long enough for them to hit, were crafted to break me. And they did, piece by piece. Each exchange left me feeling smaller, as if his ultimate goal was to make me disappear entirely.

Or, worse, to beg for it all to stop - to beg to return, because things were so much easier if I just gave in. If I just complied.

In Enrico's world, that breakfast we had wasn't a gesture of kindness. It wasn't about returning my laptop. It was a calculated experiment, another concept in his endless theatre of control, a new trap to draw me back in. The setting was comfortable, too comfortable, and beneath it all, I could feel the tension, the underlying current that never let up.

About half an hour into our meal, Enrico's iPhone lit up. An incoming call. A mature Middle Eastern woman's face appeared on the screen, attempting a smile. It was Dina Aslan.

What followed was a performance I hadn't anticipated. He didn't answer. A casual swipe, rejection. His face remained unreadable. A moment passed, and Dina called again. Persistent. Relentless. Enrico rolled his eyes, muttered something about how impossible she was, and dismissed the call again. I watched, silently taking it in.

Then two more calls. Quick. Sharp. Ignored. Dismissed.

Finally, he blocked her. Just like that. A few taps, and Dina was gone. Profile deleted. Erased.

I raised an eyebrow, dryly noting, "Looks like you've found exactly what you're after. A two-way chase." The words hung there for a beat, and I saw the flicker in his eyes, the slight narrowing, as if debating whether to let me further in on this game.

He started talking, slowly at first, about how hard she was to shake off. How she didn't get the message. How she clung. Her accent, her pushiness, her constant neediness - all of it was laid bare like evidence. I was meant to be part of the inside joke now, the confidante laughing with him.

We joked. We picked apart the image of her face. We dissected her supposed desperation.

But underneath it all, it wasn't about Dina. It was about me.

To Enrico, Dina fought. She called. She chased. She refused to let go. She wanted him.

And I? I sat across from him, detached. I didn't fight. I took him to court. I threw him out. I turned away. His words weren't just criticism - they were a challenge, a plea, a punishment. Why wasn't I more like her? Why didn't I fight for him?

This breakfast wasn't a peace offering. It was bait. And it led me straight back to his apartment.

Later, I found out just how deep the setup ran. Dina wasn't some random woman harassing him. She was part of the design. Enrico had been using his son, John Paul Pucci, as a convenient shield to keep Dina away, spinning stories about his children moving in, about needing space, about his "new chapter in life." It was the perfect excuse to see her only when it suited him.

He controlled her, entertained her, on his terms. When he wanted her, he reached out. When he didn't, she was kept at bay by excuses, by manipulated text messages signed under John Paul's name.

What kind of messages?

Whatever it took. The sky was his limit.

It was clear that Dina and Enrico were operating on entirely different wavelengths when it came to their relationship. For

Enrico, Dina served a purpose. She wasn't someone he genuinely cared about; she was an accessory, a living trophy, a placeholder that validated him. She was proof that he was desirable, wanted, proof he could wield like a weapon to manipulate me - or anyone - into believing the narrative he needed to sell.

Dina, to put it plainly, was what Australians would call a rebound. A temporary fixture, someone to fill the void. But Dina didn't seem to grasp that reality. She clung to an idea, something she believed to be real. For her, it wasn't fleeting. She saw something deeper, even as Enrico worked hard to keep her at arm's length. It was painful to watch - two people stuck on different planets, with no bridge between them.

And then there was me.

I didn't want anything more. I didn't need anything more. I just needed my stuff.

I was desperate to move on.

Desperate enough to pass the "Enrico virus" to its next host. I was done trying to rescue it all. I needed to rescue myself.

No, meeting Enrico didn't help me get my belongings. I came home empty-handed. Again.

I had no money to buy a new laptop. I didn't even have money to buy clothes. I was living in my daughter's hand-me-downs, clothes stretched thin, with holes in all the places that seemed to gather the most displaced water - or fat, if I'm honest.

I had no money. Full stop.

As I left Enrico's apartment that day, he began his usual interrogation - where was I living now, who was I with, what was my address? I rushed for the door, fully aware that the longer I stayed, the more danger I was in. The berating would begin, the threats, maybe even something worse. I knew that giving him my address would mean the end of any shred of safety I still had.

It was paramount that Enrico did not know where I lived. Paramount.

I even changed Kamron's school to keep him from following us home. It turned our lives upside down, caused a massive disruption in Kamron's world, but it had to be done.

Leaving Enrico's apartment took four modes of transport. Four. And the entire time, I worried he might be following me. Enrico co-managed a security business. He had resources, people, ways to track anyone. Especially me.

A few days later, he called. We spoke again. He was everywhere - remorseful one moment, detached the next. His words slurred; he sounded medicated, barely coherent. Then my mum's phone rang - loud, insistent. She was sitting next to me in the tiny studio I was renting under Shirina's name.

Enrico paused. "Whose phone is that? Wow, you're with someone, aren't you? You've moved on. Just like that. No looking back, ever."

And then came the rage. Yelling so loud I couldn't hear myself think. Accusations hurled at full volume, a wave of noise I couldn't cut through. I didn't try to explain. I didn't owe him an explanation. All I knew was that this was another door closing, another chance lost to get my things back.

What followed was another spiral. More drama. More noise.

Emails flooded in - begging, pleading for me to marry him, to forget everything, to start fresh. He couldn't stand the idea that I might have moved on. That I could leave him behind while he was still stuck, still trying to pull me back. The fact that using Dina - or any of the other women - hadn't worked only made it worse. It ate him alive.

And then he went further. He found a wedding celebrant. Filled out applications. Coordinated meetings. Paid deposits for photography, flowers, the celebrant. He even booked a date - November 18, 2020. Everything carefully staged, laid out in writing, unfolding right in front of me.

But I'd seen this before.

Faking bowel cancer. Pretending to talk to doctors, nurses, anyone on the phone - conversations that never happened. Lying about his passport, about deposits for our home. Every promise, every gesture, a meticulously crafted illusion.

This wedding? Just another elaborate hoax.

A new bubble, designed just for me. Another trap.

Two days before the wedding, I cut off all communication. I got a new number. I really don't know how exactly Enrico killed his time or his sorrow after that. Dina, however, provided a series of scenarios later. None of them can be relied upon objectively, as you will find out in later chapters - if you choose to stay with me long enough.

Now, how far would you go to survive? Let's revisit the opening paragraph of this chapter.

How deep does self-preservation run in our veins? Survival quickly becomes a series of simple equations to me. Like heat equals life. Food equals strength. Complacency equals death.

The subject of survival becomes prominent after the 7th of December 2020, some 21 days after my last interaction with Enrico.

On the 7th of December 2020, I received a text message from a Frank, sent from an unknown number. Frank advised me that Enrico had moved to Melbourne, Victoria, and left my belongings in boxes for Frank to deliver back to me. I responded, instructing Frank to leave my property at my old address in Willoughby with my ex-neighbour, Ritu. I provided the address. Frank replied that his instructions were to deliver the boxes to me in person, and he had limited time left with the rented van that contained my belongings.

The lingering thought of finally coming out of my daughter's clothes and putting my own on, giving my mother her robes and slippers, my son his swimmers, and being able to wear my lens and read - overtook me. I gave in. I provided Frank with my address and asked him to leave the boxes in the foyer. He replied he could not do that; he was instructed to hand the boxes over to me in person for security reasons.

I provided him with a time slot to arrive and hand over the boxes in person. Later, I received an SMS notifying me that he was downstairs with the boxes.

I went downstairs - and there he was.

Enrico.

With a bunch of flowers. No van. No boxes. No Frank.

Enrico and I had a fight. He told me he was done with Dina Aslan and wanted to rekindle with me. He claimed he wanted to fix things between us, return my property, and to prove his sincerity, he provided me with Dina's email address should I wish to validate his claim. The email address, as I later discovered, was incorrect.

Out of unexpected charity, he also left his Apple iPad for my son, Kamron.

Later, while looking at Kamron's iPad after Enrico left, I discovered the device was fully linked and tapped into Enrico's mainstream communication platforms. His entire digital world lay open in front of me. I traced back Enrico's romantic conversations with a multitude of women - as far as I could.

I was profoundly angry.

Angry at the ploy. Angry at the sheer sophistication of it. Angry at myself for being so utterly stupid, for letting this happen to me.

I came to learn I was just another number in a much bigger scheme. There were a lot of numbers. I stood out - yes, I did. I was the longest affair. I was the most vulnerable number of all. I had no males in my family to stand up for me. I had dependants. I wasn't mobile, and I was too senior, too visible, to take "dramatic" steps in my self-defence.

Anger filled every pore of my existence at the thought of what happened to my life - how I was left to camp in a studio, sharing a king bed with my mother and son, at my lowest.

Anger consumed my thoughts, my actions, my reactions, as I read through besotted messages from women lining up to date and mate with rich and famous Enrico Pucci.

And of them, Dina Aslan stood out like a sore eye.

I became privy to the revolting, relentless exchange of sexually charged images and messages between Enrico Pucci and Dina Aslan.

But it didn't stop there.

Their exchange included something else - something darker. Menacing intent towards me. Subtle, constant. A symphony of cruelty played between them. Conversations planning how they would bankrupt me. Remove my son from my care. Catch me in breach of a non-existing AVO against me. Destroy my property still in Enrico's possession. The threats were endless.

I couldn't hold it anymore.

There was so much pent-up pain, so much resentment, that I entered the most heartfelt, rageful, and uncontrollable exchange with Dina Aslan.

Her sarcastic responses to my emails? They felt like she was getting a kick out of it. Getting off on the fact that she was in a relationship built on the back of my destruction.

And here I was again! Welcome back into the vortex of hundreds of exes manipulated in and out of sexual or romantic relationships with Enrico Pucci. A man who carefully crafts his image, swapping partners like gloves, he transforms himself every time he enters a room, radiating an aura of importance. This air of significance is enough to draw countless women into his orbit, many lured by the allure of his wealth and status. His presence is magnetic, his influence insidious, and his charm convincingly real.

No, you cannot raincheque your way out of this twisted cycle. Once he knows your address, your life becomes entangled in his web. There is no pause, no escape. You are in it. Full stop.

Emotional and physical extortion are tools in his arsenal, ensuring that even those who try to leave are brought back into his dangerous game. It's a game without boundaries, without commitment, and with no clear exit. You are left trapped in a relentless cycle of manipulation, a pawn in his never-ending pursuit of control.

So, the plan. Yes, brewed up a plan.

The grand plan.

It previously changed from fear to fight. And I did win. Or I thought so. I secured an Apprehended Violence Order against Enrico in April 2020, and the Judgment to pay me back my 100,000 AUD around the same time. Neither is worth the paper they were written on. Having an Order simply does not equal having the Order complied with. I could hang them on my wall as my achievements, but the net effect of me being manipulated and exploited day in and day out of my life by a man not my size remained unchanged.

Yes, the plan.

It changed again on the 7th of December 2020. It morphed from fight to flight. "Flight" became my new modus operandi.

Three years later, in late 2022, I started working with a psychologist to revisit these events and unpack my responses. She introduced me to the concept of the Fear-Fight-Fawn (Flight) response, using it as a framework to explain how my reactions followed patterns seen in countless others facing similar situations. She explained that these responses are deeply embedded in human psychology, an evolutionary blueprint designed to protect us in moments of extreme stress, danger, or despair.

At first, I was surprised by how predictable my reactions seemed when viewed through this lens. It was fascinating to realize that what felt so personal and unique to me was actually part of a shared human experience, a survival mechanism that has been widely studied and understood. Yet, at the same time, I couldn't help but feel there was something extraordinary about what I chose to do next. It was as if I had tapped into an inner strength or instinct that I didn't know I had, even though, from a psychological standpoint, it was completely expected.

The states of fear, fight, and flight are part of the body's natural stress response, often referred to as the "fight-or-flight response." This response is triggered by the autonomic nervous system when we perceive a threat or danger.

- **What It Is:** Fear is the emotional and physiological reaction to a perceived threat. It acts as the trigger for the fight-or-flight response.
  Purpose: Fear is a survival mechanism that helps us recognize and respond to potential threats. It primes the body to either confront the danger (fight) or escape it (flight).
- **What It Is:** The "fight" response is the body's preparation to confront and combat the threat head-on.
  Purpose: This response is useful when the threat is something that can be overcome through confrontation, such as defending oneself from an attacker.

- **What It Is:** The "flight" response is the body's preparation to escape the threat and seek safety.
  Fawn: In some cases, individuals may respond by trying to appease the threat, often seen in social or interpersonal conflicts, or immerse themselves in a character or experience for the sake of survival.
  Purpose: This response is ideal when the threat is too overwhelming or dangerous to confront, making escape or immersion the safest option.

Yes, the plan was to immerse myself in Enrico's life and see him arrested. My plan was to lock him up to attain my freedom and the time needed for me to reconstruct my life.

No, I saw no other solution to my situation. No. No one else could help or care. I was in it alone.

The Plan: The Wedding

On the 6th of June 2021, I stood still, facing wedding celebrant number four. We are in Observatory Hill Park, tucked behind the historic Sydney Observatory Building. It's 11 am. The park is beautiful and serene, a hidden gem in the heart of the Sydney CBD. Despite its seclusion, it carries an air of prestige, a prime location for such an occasion. My witness is my mother, standing quietly by my side, her expression unreadable. Meanwhile, my young boy runs around the park, collecting twigs and leaves, completely oblivious to the significance of the day. In his happy-go-lucky world, this is just another adventure in the park. The air is crisp, with the unmistakable bite of a cold winter's day. I clutch my jacket tightly, bracing against the chill.

The celebrant, a cheerful woman with a radiant smile, seems eager to proceed. She is the only person in attendance who carries a palpable sense of joy. In her hand is a bottle of champagne, ready to pop in celebration of the event, a thoughtful gesture that feels somewhat out of place given the circumstances. She seems genuinely invested in making this day special, even as she stands amidst an audience that feels heavy with unspoken tension and sadness. This is not the kind of wedding she is probably used to officiating, but she carries on with professionalism and a forced cheerfulness.

But there's one glaring issue: there is no groom in sight. "Enrico is late," she says, her smile unwavering as she tries to maintain composure.

"No, he's not," I reply, my voice calm but hollow.

At that moment, the trunk of my old Toyota Camry, a 2000 model, pops open. From inside, Enrico climbs out, his movements stiff as he adjusts to the cold air and stretches his limbs. The celebrant's smile falters slightly as confusion washes over her face. Her eyes dart between me, Enrico, and the trunk. A thousand questions seem to cross her mind, but she holds them back, perhaps sensing this is not the time for explanations. The setup resembles an exchange point between two mafia gangs, where one must exercise utmost care for their life because they are wanted by rival gangs. To complete the picture, Enrico is missing his cane engraved with a golden handle in which he holds a stash of diamonds, or something equally precious many would risk their lives for.

The celebrant appears intuitive enough to grasp the situation quickly. She registers the weight of the moment; the air is heavy, the silence thick and oppressive. No one is smiling except her, and even her smile has started to waver. My mother shifts uncomfortably while my son continues to play, blissfully unaware of the tension surrounding him.

The celebrant seems to understand that this wedding is not just about love or celebration. There is a necessity for it. There is formality. We are here to tick the boxes, to get this over with as quickly as possible.

My heart feels heavy, and I can't help but wonder how we got here to this strange and sombre moment. I glance at Enrico, whose face is a mixture of impatience and anxiety. He shouldn't even be here, not even for his own wedding. He's on bail. His existence is confined to the four walls of his father's residence by a court order. This act of rebellion, sneaking out to get married, carries significant risks, and the sooner we conclude it, the safer it will be for him.

No, his family does not know he is with me. They don't know he is getting married or risking his freedom by standing next to me. This book will not explore the ins and outs of what it took Enrico to get into the trunk of my car. What resources, people, and means he utilised to get out of his father's residence, which is presently serving as his jail facility according to his latest bail conditions.

Enrico is officially in home-bound incarceration in the comfort of his father's house.

The celebrant takes it all in, appearing to adjust gracefully to the bizarre circumstances. She explains that she brought a friend along at the request of Enrico to serve as a witness to this event. And the friend is confined to the confidentiality of the event until such time Enrico consents for the event to become public.

She begins the secret ceremony, her voice steady and professional, though the light-heartedness she initially brought seems to have faded. The champagne bottle remains unopened in her hand.

Enrico and I exchange our vows, his voice steady and filled with emotion as he speaks the words. These vows were prepared and submitted by Enrico, carefully thought out to reflect our journey together through his lens. The celebrant smiles as she declares us husband and wife. She pops open a bottle of champagne and shares the glasses of champagne around.

Enrico is restless, his eyes darting across the park as if searching for something or someone. He takes a quick sip of champagne, then downs the rest in one swift motion, his anxiety palpable. He glances at me expectantly, silently urging me to do the same as though finishing the champagne would signal the conclusion of this moment. I hesitate for a moment, letting the significance of the day sink in before bringing the glass to my lips. The soft hum of nature surrounds us, blending with the laughter of a few distant strangers as the weight of the day begins to settle on both of us.

I am now officially the wife of the Italian Mafia-Con; I am Narghiza Ergashova Pucci.

Enrico climbs back into the trunk of my car. He is unaware that I was the reason his bail conditions were tightened just weeks ago, on the 26th of May 2021, to be precise. My reports to various authorities were the reason behind the surge in police pursuit and attendance.

Enrico Pucci was arrested on the 4th of February 2021 and released on bail for driving while disqualified. Narghiza Ergashova reported Enrico Pucci to police, describing in detail the motor vehicle he was driving and the direction he was heading.

Enrico Pucci was arrested again on the 26th of May 2021 and released on bail for driving while disqualified; Gloria Edmonds, another ex-lover of Enrico, reported him by providing CCTV footage, engaging her friend, who was part of the strata committee in the building block, to police after Narghiza Ergashova provided her with all the details.

Yet Narghiza's mission remains incomplete. It was not enough to keep Enrico on bail at home. Narghiza's plan was to see him behind bars at a correctional facility. A proper corrective facility.

In exchange, Enrico gets exactly what he wants: total perceived control over Narghiza Ergashova. Narghiza Ergashova dedicates her life to him. So much so that in January 2022, she plans his biggest 46th birthday ever! It is so big it hits the Australian news charts!

The Plan: After The Wedding

Enrico and I moved in together a few days after getting married. We move into the 35th floor of the luxurious apartment block on Bathurst Street, Sydney CBD. The apartment is a state-of-the-art residence with panoramic views of Sydney CBD from various angles. Enrico successfully applies for his bail variation, where he is allowed to reside with me, his wife, Narghiza Ergashova, at his new address. Enrico is still in home incarceration pending his final hearing for disqualified driving.

On the surface, I seem to be blissfully settled. We are in the middle of the COVID pandemic, and our residence is just about the best place to be locked in, spacious, quiet, and with enviable views of the surrounding cityscape. Those views, however, come with a unique perspective on the strange and often grim realities of the pandemic. Among the sights is the infamous quarantine hotel, located opposite our building. The hotel is a temporary refuge for incoming travellers who, regardless of their residency status, were legally required to isolate for fourteen days before being allowed to re-enter society. The hotel, while designed as a place of confinement, was a hub of relentless activity, offering a stark contrast to the stillness of the world outside.

Through the expansive glass walls of our living room and balcony, we observed a parade of human drama. The hotel became a stage for desperation, with some individuals climbing onto the roof in tragic attempted suicides, their despair palpable even from our distant vantage point. Others harmed themselves within the confines of their rooms, leading to a near-constant presence of ambulances and fire trucks parked at the base of the building. It wasn't unusual to see emergency responders springing into action every other day, their flashing lights and wailing sirens breaking the eerie quiet of the streets below.

Amid this chaos, there were also moments of bizarre intimacy. Occasionally, isolated guests would engage in passionate, unfiltered exchanges of intense intercourse, with curtains and windows left wide open. These displays, while uncomfortable and oddly voyeuristic, were in some ways a grim reminder of the need for human connection in even the most challenging of circumstances. Strangely enough, these encounters were sometimes preferred to the others, far darker scenes that unfolded within the hotel. The glass walls that surrounded us served as a lens through which we witnessed the raw, unvarnished reality of life during a pandemic, chaotic, heartbreaking, and oddly surreal.

Inside, however, I felt dead. It wasn't a sudden death but something that had happened a long time ago, piece by piece, like a slow erosion of everything that made me human. Being dead, in a way, was comforting. It stripped away the chaos of emotions and left me with a singular focus: my plan. My plan was simple but invasive, and it left no room for doubt or hesitation. It involved breaking into Enrico's devices, diving deep into his digital life, and uncovering every secret he thought was safe. I tuned into all his conversations, sifted through every drawer and cupboard, read every message he sent or received, and analysed his exchanges and transactions.

The more I dug, the more I unravelled the threads of Enrico's life. Little by little, I was piecing him together in ways no one else ever had. His patterns, his choices, his secrets - they were all laid bare before me. It was like building a puzzle of a man who thought he was untraceable, but I was determined to know him better than he knew himself.

One night, Enrico was sound asleep in a deep, almost unshakable slumber. I lay in bed next to him, my heart pounding with anticipation, waiting patiently to hear the steady rhythm of his snores. When they finally came, soft but distinct, I knew it was time. I shifted slightly in bed, tossing lightly to see if he would stir. He didn't. His breathing remained even and undisturbed.

Slowly, I slid the covers off, careful not to make a sound. I didn't dare stand up, fearing the creak of the wooden floorboards beneath the carpets under my feet might betray me. Instead, I lowered myself to the ground and crawled like a toddler, my palms and knees pressing into the carpet as I moved inch by inch toward Enrico's bedside table. My breath hitched when I reached it, the faint glow of his charging iPhone catching my eye. My hands hesitated for a brief moment before I grabbed it, the weight of the device feeling heavier than it should in my trembling fingers.

I backed away from the table, still crawling, my heart hammering in my chest. Every movement felt slow and deliberate, like I was in a heist movie. Each sound, even the softest creak, seemed deafening in the silence. Clutching the phone tightly, I finally made it to the door. I gently slipped outside the bedroom with the phone in my hands.

My plan was simple but nerve-wracking: I needed to gather as much information as I could. Sifting through everything in life while in his presence wasn't practical. Asleep or not, it was too risky. I needed the information "downloaded" first, in the form of images, so I could analyze it later in detail, away from the pressure of discovery. In the darkened hallway, I sat down, unlocked his phone, and began scrolling. I scoured through his communications, messages, emails, and social media chats and flipped through his photo gallery, documents, and anything else I could find that might give me the answers I was looking for. My hands were trembling, both from fear and adrenaline, as I worked quickly.

I took thousands of photos with my own phone as I scrolled through his, snapping screenshots of everything. Sometimes, the images were blurry or crooked because my hands were unsteady or I was rushing too much. The pressure of the moment was overwhelming. What if he woke up? What if he caught me? My mind raced with worst-case scenarios as I hurried to capture as much as I could before his peaceful slumber ended.

The silence of the house only made things worse. The faint hum of the refrigerator in the other room and the occasional groan of the old building felt deafening in the quiet. Every second felt like an eternity as I worked, my stomach twisting in knots of fear and panic. I didn't have time to double-check what I was capturing; that would have to come later. Right now, all I could do was move fast and hope I wouldn't miss anything important.

I panicked, my mind constantly cycling between staying calm and wanting to flee back to bed. I couldn't stop now. I had to see this through. I had to know. I had to...

I had many similar nights that saw me prowl around the corners of the apartment in pitch dark. I did not live. I existed.

Cracking the Pucci Code – Take One

- **The Syndicate**

  The Pucci brothers, whether by conscious design or subconscious conditioning from their background, operated as part of an organized syndicate with a unified purpose: the romantic and financial exploitation of women. Their methods, refined over time, reflected a deliberate, almost business-like approach to manipulation.

- **The Women: Marginalized and Targeted**

  Each woman they pursued shared a common vulnerability - marginalization by race, origin, age, or limited access to essential resources like legal protection or financial independence. Below are non-exhaustive examples illustrating their reach:

a. **[Enrico Pucci] - Narghiza Ergashova**

$100k debt, lured with promises of marriage and cohabitation in a luxury apartment in Walsh Bay, Sydney, NSW. **[Substantiated]**

b. [Enrico Pucci] - Dina Aslan

$500k debt, lured with promises of marriage and life together in a Millers Point penthouse, Sydney NSW. **[Partly Substantiated]**

c. [Enrico Pucci] - Gloria Edmonds

$250k prospective debt, with similar promises of marriage and living in Elysium, a luxury apartment block on the Gold Coast, QLD. **[Speculative]**

d. [Ross Pucci] - Patrizia Fontera

Business MOU combined with multiple attempts to initiate a romantic relationship. **[Speculative]**

e. [Ross Pucci] - Liliana Freedman

Possible business MOU and romantic involvement. **[Speculative]**

f. [Ross Pucci] - Juliana Bond

Possible business MOU; currently remains in a romantic relationship with Ross Pucci. **[Speculative]**

- **The Strategies of Exploitation**

  Their methods were systematic, falling into four distinct categories:

a. Money as Leverage

Enrico Pucci used his perceived wealth and influence - his ostentatious lifestyle, supposed powerful networks, and exaggerated financial standing - to impress, seduce, and control.

b. Health as Manipulation

Enrico's fabricated illnesses, including staged seizures and dramatized health crises (real or fake), became tools of gaslighting. He used on-demand medical emergencies, suicidal threats, and emotional collapse to manipulate, delay, and trap women emotionally.

c. Comparative Devaluation / Inflated Superiority

Enrico employed psychological warfare by inflating each woman's sense of superiority. He degraded Narghiza Ergashova, painting her as obsessed and destructive, promising other women they were his saviours, the ones who would replace her and see her downfall.

d. False Impressions and Identity Manipulation

His phones were a maze of deception:

Random women were labelled as "Narghiza Ergashova," allowing him to show staged calls that reinforced the narrative of an obsessed ex chasing him.

Narghiza herself was marked as "Nina from Cancer Care," creating an excuse for him to take her calls in front of others, masquerading them as medical-related.

This illusion of being pursued by a crazy ex, while also fighting terminal illness, made Enrico irresistible - a tragic, wealthy hero in need of saving.

- **The Web of Deceit**

  All women were aware of Narghiza Ergashova's role in Enrico's life, presented to them as the high-profile obsessed villain in his narrative. What they didn't know - or couldn't confirm - was that they were just one of many. Each woman was isolated in her knowledge, some suspecting others but never truly grasping the scale.

Side Note on Nina from Cancer Care

Let's step back for a moment, returning to that chapter where Enrico's bowel cancer and multiple sclerosis were central to the story he crafted. Do you remember how thoroughly I believed it?

How deeply was I drawn into the web of his so-called terminal illness? He painted it vividly - the pain, the fatigue, the slow decline - and I followed every word, desperate to support him. A key figure in this story was Belinda, his "nurse," the one who was supposedly by his side throughout the darkest parts of his diagnosis. On his phone, she was saved as "Belinda – Cancer Care."

Enrico treated these calls with Belinda like sacred rites. Whenever her name popped up on his screen, he would snap to attention. His body language shifted: alert, solemn, consumed by what seemed like life-altering information. He'd rush out of the room, taking the call in private, leaving me behind in a whirlwind of fear and sympathy. He'd return moments later, his face heavy with supposed grief, detailing the latest turn for the worse - new symptoms, harsher treatments, bleaker prospects.

He was so convincing.

At one point, I was meant to meet Belinda. Of course, I wanted to. As his fiancée, how could I not want to meet the woman who was guiding him through his illness? But that meeting never happened. Every time it was about to, something came up. Belinda had emergencies. Or the timing wasn't right. Or Enrico himself would decide it wasn't necessary. Each excuse sounded reasonable. Each excuse kept me in the dark.

And now? Now I see what I couldn't see then. It was all fabrication, every last bit.

Because Belinda wasn't a nurse. Belinda was his wife.

Belinda Pucci. The same woman he claimed was out of his life was still very much in it.

They weren't living together. Maybe. Or maybe they were. Maybe he spun her a different tale, about expanding his business, about being busy interstate. The truth? They spoke regularly. They were still entangled, while I was caught in the same web - unaware, just like her.

That number on his phone, marked as "Belinda – Cancer Care", wasn't a nurse at all.

It was Belinda Pucci.

And me?

I was "Nina – From Cancer Care."

That's what he saved my number as.

Do you see it now?

He played both of us. Day in and day out, for more than two and a half years. We were both fooled, believing we were the central figures in his life, when in truth, we were characters in his ever-evolving script. Belinda even reached out a few times, calling me from private numbers, but she never allowed for a comprehensive conversation to occur. She hung up after spitting out a few words at me. Maybe she sensed something. Maybe she didn't. We never had the chance to connect, to share notes, to escape together from the man who bound us in this cycle of lies.

But here it is - the truth, plain and brutal:

He was still married.

And he was engaged to me all that time.

Cracking the Code – Take Two

1. The Pucci Brothers: A Legacy of Kiss-and-Tell Bravado

The Puccis weren't just brothers - they were competitors. Their scandalous romantic pursuits weren't merely about desire or affection; they were status symbols, carefully selected trophies meant to outshine one another. The more ambitious the woman - by background, beauty, or social standing - the more valuable she became in this twisted game of one-upmanship. Each conquest was less about the woman herself and more about bragging rights. Who could seduce the most unattainable? Who could manipulate the most devoted?

2. **Refer to Points Two and Three**

As outlined previously, exploitation was strategic, and targets shared common vulnerabilities - age, race, financial status, or isolation from legal recourse.

3. **A Façade of Wealth over Financial Ruin**

Behind the designer clothes, flashy cars, and luxury apartments was a mountain of debt. The Puccis were in financial freefall, yet they orchestrated an illusion of abundance. Credit lines, unpaid invoices, and borrowed riches were the real architects of their opulence. The wealth they flaunted didn't exist - it was a mirage, carefully maintained to draw in those who believed in the fantasy.

4. **No Real Power, Just Intimidation**

Their talk of underworld ties and criminal networks was just that - talk. The threats, the boasts, the shadows they cast, all designed to frighten those who couldn't call their bluff. Migrant women, particularly, were easy targets: without connections, without protection, they were vulnerable. The Puccis thrived on fear, spinning tales of power they didn't possess to control those they could.

Women as Tokens in a Brotherly Contest

It wasn't about love. It wasn't even about lust. For the Puccis, women were objects, used not to gain public admiration but to impress each other. Every relationship was a move on a chessboard, every lie a tactic to prove superiority within their private, toxic rivalry.

Petty Criminals in Designer Suits

They weren't mafia. They weren't masterminds. They were small-time players with big-time delusions. Petty criminals who dressed up their cons with theatrics and bravado, pretending to be sharks while swimming with minnows. But like all illusions, this too would shatter - because fish tanks aren't oceans, and eventually, even the biggest fish in a small tank gets exposed.

Cracking the Code – Take Three

1. All Points from Take Two Stand Firm

The illusion of power, the façade of wealth, the brotherly competition, the manipulation of women - nothing changes from Take Two. The groundwork of exploitation and ego-driven deceit remains, but the picture broadens.

2. The Pucci-Cons Meet Their Match

The infamous kiss-and-tell brothers - the self-styled kings of manipulation - hit a nerve they never anticipated. They stumbled into a web bigger, more intricate, and far more dangerous than their own petty schemes. What they unleashed was not just retaliation from the women they had wronged, but the wrath of a more sophisticated machine - one that played a different game entirely.

Dina Aslan wasn't just another number in Enrico's playbook. She became the architect of something larger. With social and legal "engineering", she stitched out of this world stories not just in private whispers but through carrier services, through the media, through channels meant to destroy reputations and reshape realities. Allegations grew beyond the usual personal revenge. It was systemic - crafted, calculated, weaponized.

3. Enrico Pucci: Victim of His Own Sword

"Those who live by the sword, die by it." Enrico lived by lies - by manipulation, control, and falsehood. His entire world was constructed on the premise that he could outsmart, outplay, and outlast. But in the end, it was his own web that ensnared him.

He was a master manipulator, but even masters fall when they can no longer see the limits of their own power.

He didn't just fall prey to others - he was undone by the very tools he used on everyone else.

The Path to Take Three: Learning the Hard Way

Reaching this third layer of truth wasn't accidental - it was inevitable. But it came at a cost. A cost so personal, so consuming, that it left me questioning whether truth was worth the ruin it brought with it.

You can't see clearly through shattered glass - and during Code One and Two, that's exactly what I tried to do.

I was desperate for patterns, for connections, for something that made sense in a world that had been twisted beyond recognition. I forced the dots to connect, driven by betrayal, clawing at the wreckage, trying to stitch logic into chaos. Every document, every blurry photo, every conversation was a piece I tried to fit into a puzzle that didn't even have edges yet. Trauma blurred everything. My mind wasn't just clouded - it was scorched, burned by the heat of anger, pain, and relentless obsession.

And then there was the bias. Mine, yes. But it wasn't just mine.

I wasn't alone in my rage. I wasn't the only one Enrico had broken, bent, and discarded. Ex-lovers. Ex-friends. Allies who hated him as much as I did. People who swore they were helping, but their help was poisoned by vengeance. They didn't want clarity - they wanted blood. They wanted to see him bleed like they had, and they used my grief as a weapon just as much as he did.

Their truths, colored red with their own wounds, mixed with mine. And suddenly, I wasn't sure whose voice I was hearing in my head anymore. Was it mine? Was it theirs? Or was it just an echo of everything I was too exhausted to fight against?

I was not fit to piece Enrico together - not then. Not while I was still bleeding.

I didn't see him clearly. I didn't see myself clearly. And the more I tried, the more I lost.

December 2022: The Final Piece Falls Into Place

Everything changed when Enrico returned.

It wasn't just about gathering information anymore - it was about understanding. About seeing the man, the myth, the manipulator, and the victim. Because by now, it was clear: Enrico was a product of his own design, but even he didn't see the whole picture.

To crack this code, you had to let him back in - not for love, not for reconciliation, but for truth. He didn't realize it, but he became part of his own undoing, giving you access not just to his life but to the last missing pieces.

And with those pieces, the full picture emerged. Clear. Inevitable. Complete.

Who am I?

14th of March 2022. Just another day. Or so I thought.

The morning had unfolded like any other - breakfast, our familiar back-and-forth filling the space with something resembling normalcy. Enrico was calm, even light-hearted, his voice carrying that casual charm he wore like a second skin. Nothing in his demeanor hinted at what was to come.

I left the apartment as I always did, moving through the mechanical routine of urban living. Leaving wasn't just slipping out the door; it was a process. The building we lived in wasn't ordinary. The first in Australia with its Japanese-engineered car stacker, a marvel of space efficiency. We'd once admired it like tourists in our own home, intrigued by its novelty. It was the kind of modern solution cities needed: compact, sleek, and cutting-edge.

But as time passed, that marvel became more of a ritual. Each morning: enter the code, swipe the pass, and wait - sometimes impatiently - as the machine whirred and groaned, pulling cars like toys from some giant metal puzzle. Some days, the wait felt like a metaphor for my life - circling, stalling, waiting for things to align.

Not today.

Today, the machine worked like clockwork. My car appeared within minutes, and I slipped behind the wheel, easing into the traffic on Elizabeth Street, thinking only about errands, about work, about anything but what was waiting.

Seven and a half minutes. That's how long I was gone when everything changed.

My phone lit up. Enrico.

I didn't hesitate - I never did when he called. But the moment I picked up, something was different. His voice wasn't his own. It trembled, cracked, unraveled.

"They're taking me in, baby," he gasped. The words spilled out like panic made flesh.

I gripped the steering wheel, my heart slamming into my ribs. "What? Who? Enrico, what's happening?"

"It's over. They're here. I'm done. I'm not coming back."

I could barely breathe. My mind raced, but my body acted first.

"I'm coming back," I said, like a reflex, like it would fix something.

But even as I turned the car around, I knew. Not in my head, but somewhere deeper - in that place where truth sits like a stone you can't swallow.

I thought - no, I hoped - this was just like before. That somehow he'd find a way out, charm the system the way he always did. Bail, excuses, a story. Back home by dinner.

But when I walked into that apartment, everything felt… still. Too still.

The air was heavy, the silence thick. No Enrico.

Just a piece of paper.

It sat there on the kitchen benchtop like it owned the room. I didn't want to touch it, but my eyes wouldn't let go. A warrant. Signed and sealed by Constable W from Paddington Police Station.

I stood there, staring at the paper. Waiting for it to change. For it to say something different.

But it didn't.

This time, he wasn't coming back.

The apartment felt hollow. Not just empty of his voice, or his footsteps echoing down the hallway, but of something deeper. The absence of him filled the room like a fog. His energy, his chaos - it had always filled every corner, pushing and pulling at my sanity, but now that it was gone, there was just this - a stillness that didn't comfort, but suffocated.

I sat at the dining table, the one meant for six. It was too big now. Too much space for just one. I didn't move. Couldn't. Time didn't pass normally anymore. Hours blurred, dissolved, and became meaningless. I was stuck - between relief and something I couldn't quite name. The silence wrapped around me like a cold blanket, heavy and unmoving, pressing down harder with every second.

This time, he wasn't just gone. He might not come back.

The court hearing for bail was scheduled for the next day. District Court, Sydney CBD. The city that had watched us spin in circles for years now held the power to decide whether the circle would close for good.

The courtroom felt colder than usual, or maybe that was just me, bracing for what I already sensed.

The lawyer representing him was a stranger. Dry, detached, like she'd seen too many of these cases to care anymore. She didn't know him. Didn't know me. She didn't see any of it. To her, he was just another file on the desk.

Her advice was mechanical: *"Apply to the Supreme Court. Request a surety. A substantial one."*

Surety. A word that tasted bitter in my mouth. Because I knew - it wouldn't be simple. It never was.

Packing his things wasn't a task - it was a reckoning. Every item I touched carried weight, memory, lies. This was it. The end we had talked around for so long but never really faced. A bittersweet freedom.

I folded his shirts like they were strangers' clothes, not the fabric of the life I'd wrapped myself in for too long. Box after box, his presence shrank, became something containable. I needed it to be containable. I needed to reclaim my space, my breath.

When I was done, I called his father.

"Would you take his things? Store them, just until - "

"No." The answer was quick. Decisive. Final.

I stood there, phone still in hand, staring into the boxes. Dumbfounded.

Ross wanted nothing to do with him - not in business, not even in the same state.

His father wouldn't have his belongings near the house.

His children? Ghosts. Estranged and silent.

And me?

I was packed, too. Ready.

I could leave him, finally, like everyone else already had. Abandon him. Walk away. Let the law keep him now. Let the silence stay.

But I couldn't shake the truth - he was truly alone. Not just left behind, but erased.

And that… that cut deeper than I ever expected.

While I packed up what was left of Enrico's life, chaos unfolded in the courtroom. No one really knew how *State v. Enrico* would shape up. And I? I didn't know whether I was going to be used - by the prosecution, or the defense.

Both sides approached me. Both thought I'd be their leverage. And both walked away when they realized I wouldn't play the part they needed me to.

The prosecution wanted more than truth - they wanted something usable. Something clean. But what I had wouldn't just complicate their case - it threatened to undo it. The very evidence I offered didn't fit their narrative. Worse, it exposed their reliance on the only other witness they had - **Dina Aslan**.

There was one email.

Late November 2021.

Dina, desperate. Begging me.

Not just to back her up, but to go to none other than Senior Sergeant CW of Surry Hills Police Station, the charging officer, and give a false statement.

That email was a red flag - a flashing alarm that neither I nor Dina could be trusted to take the stand.

And so, just like that, both our submissions were dismissed. Erased from the proceedings. The State didn't want the mess that came with us – ex-partners. The defense didn't need the risk.

Two weeksafter Enrico was incarcerated and bail was refused for altering a medical certificate, my phone rang. Private number.

I almost didn't answer, but something in me did. Instinct, maybe. Habit.

It was Silverwater Metropolitan Remand and Correctional Complex.

A softly spoken officer introduced himself, polite to a fault. Said Enrico had been hospitalized several times in just the last two weeks. Said he was struggling. Said he wasn't doing well.

But there was one thing he wanted. One thing he pleaded for so hard, the officer decided to bend the rules - just once.

"Are you ready?" the officer asked me. My heart sank.

I braced for the worst.

Are you happy now? Are you celebrating? Are you proud?

"Yes," I said quietly, barely holding it together.

The officer paused, then spoke.

"Enrico has just one question for you… Who am I?"

I didn't think. I didn't hesitate.

"Polar Bear," I whispered.

And then louder, "You are my Polar Bear."

The officer laughed. Said that would make Enrico's day. That it would give him the strength he needed.

When Enrico came out months later, he told me the officer had passed on my answer. And with it, a comment.

"You're a lucky man. That one would last to the end. She'll see you through this."

Journey to Healing

When Enrico was taken away, my life split into two *irreconcilable* realities.

One was gleaming, untouchable - a high-tech utopia where death had been outsmarted, and time itself became a luxury good. The elite lived forever, their bodies sculpted by science, their diseases erased by nanotechnology. In their world, mortality was optional. They crafted legacies measured not in decades but in centuries, free from the decay the rest of us couldn't escape.

And then there was the other world - mine. The forgotten lands.

We weren't separated by oceans or borders but by something far more impenetrable: inequality. The kind that wasn't just about money, but about *worth*. About visibility. We lived in the shadow of their cities, watching as resources were poured into eternal life while we scrambled for another day.

It wasn't just about who had more.

It was about who mattered more.

These weren't just different lives; they were different species.

And no, the tragedy wasn't that both worlds existed. The tragedy was that we accepted them. That we learned to live side by side with this divide as though it were written in the laws of nature.

In the middle of this divide stood a fortress - a place where human beings ceased to be human at all.

A corrective facility in the heart of New South Wales. A machine designed not to correct but to reduce. A place where men became six digits. Nothing more. MIN. Master Index Numbers.

Enrico became one of them.

Twice a day, the roll call sounded. Not names. Numbers.

The officers didn't care who was hungry, who was hurting, who remembered the warmth of a family, or the cold edge of a mistake. They cared only for the count. That the system had not misplaced its liabilities.

Straight lines. Eyes front. "Here."

Tick.

At best, the roll call was a joke, a chance for power to flex itself, for officers to mock a man who didn't stand straight enough. A man who didn't wear his shame properly.

At worst, it was just empty. A routine. A system ticking over.

Each "here" wasn't a voice - it was an echo of dehumanization. Not one of them was a man anymore. Just an inventory.

Two weeks after that officer had called me with Enrico's question - *Who am I?* - my phone rang again.

It was him.

His voice was like sandpaper - raw, scraped down to the bone. I barely recognized it.

"I don't have long," he said, frantic, as though every second cost him something. Like he had to spend these words carefully.

In the background, chaos.

Not just noise. A storm.

A flood of voices - male, mostly. Shouting. Pushing. The kind of noise you feel in your chest before your ears catch up.

It was more than just unrest. It was volatile. *Something was about to break.*

Enrico's voice strained against the chaos, his words splintered by fear and violence.

"Ohh baby," he gasped - But this wasn't affection.

It was the sound of a man unraveling.

Not even a scream, just something hollow. Something dying.

Then silence.

A short breath.

And then another voice - not his.

Rough, violent, muffled. Like someone else had taken the phone. Or taken him.

What followed was the kind of shouting you feel in your chest. Not arguments. Not fights. *Threats*.

Words you don't need to decipher to understand.

Then - nothing…The call dropped.

Just silence, and the cold echo of a line that had *already heard too much*.

I sat frozen, phone pressed to my cheek, heart galloping, ears still ringing with the chaos from the other side.

It took me three months to understand what happened that day.

Three months of speculation, unanswered calls, and sporadic, censored prison letters.

Three months before I learned the full story.

Remand Isn't a Place. It's a Punishment Before the Punishment.

Enrico had been locked inside Silverwater MRCC - Silverwater *Remand*.

Let's be clear: remand doesn't mean guilty.

It means waiting.

It means being caught in limbo, a human being tossed into the bowels of a machine that doesn't care who you are or why you're there.

Remand is the graveyard of assumption.

It's where the unconvicted rot while the system decides whether to make their destruction official.

Silverwater isn't built for safety.

It's built for *containment*.

They call it a *holding* centre - but what they're holding isn't just people. It's pressure. Rage. Guilt. Desperation.

There are no classifications. No distinctions.

White-collar crimes.

Drug lords.

DV breach offenders.

Murderers.

All thrown together.

Same walls.

Same air.

Same fights.

A hardened rapist in the top bunk.

A 19-year-old first-time offender on the floor.

No system. No logic.

Just metal doors and assigned numbers.

You're either prey, or you're pretending not to be.

That broken phone call made sense when I learned what Silverwater was.

It wasn't just a bad connection.

It was a storm he had been swallowed by.

Inmates screaming not for justice, but for food.

Fighting over soap.

Over calls.

Over beds.

Over *nothing* - because in there, nothing is all you have.

And in that place, Enrico - petty criminal, manipulative as he was - was still not built for it.

He wasn't the alpha he pretended to be in the outside world.

In there, he was just another number.

Three months later, they transferred him to Clarence Correctional Centre.

A cleaner, newer facility.

More suited to offenders like him.

Less chaos, more structure.

Still prison.

But not a slaughterhouse.

And me?

I was left staring at the system - at both of us - wondering how we got here.

How a master manipulator got swallowed by the very storm he once used to control others.

And how I, the woman he buried under years of gaslighting and staged crises, had become the keeper of his truth.

If you've stayed with me this long, you've probably begun to see it too.

The gap.

The space where communication should live, but never does.

It's the silence between the screams. The hollow between the chaos.

You're not just waiting for a phone call.

You're waiting for a voice.

A voice that's trapped in a system that doesn't care if it ever reaches you.

Let me be clear: communication wasn't just hard - it was a war.

Every single word Enrico and I exchanged was fought for.

And the battle didn't start with us - it started with a wall-mounted, rusted-out relic of a phone.

One phone.

For one block.

In the largest Remand Facility in NSW.

No time slots.

No rules.

No fairness.

Just who's strongest.

Who's fastest.

Who's willing to bleed for a chance to say, *"I'm still here."*

You want to know why we couldn't talk?

Because he didn't know if he'd get to call.

Because he didn't know when he'd get pulled off the line, fists in his ribs, shanked over a minute too long.

Because even when he did get through, he didn't know how long he had.

Minutes? Seconds?

He didn't have time for explanations.

Only time to beg me to understand without them.

I remember the first time he got shanked for me.

Because he refused to hang up.

Because he wouldn't let go.

Because he chose my voice over his safety.

Let that sink in.

"Write it down."

"I can't explain."

"Just listen to me, please."

That was all he could say - between the shouting, between the fear. That wasn't conversation. That was survival pretending to be connection.

He stood in that line for me.

Every day.

That was his life - his purpose - for those three months.

Queue up. Get shoved. Bleed if you have to.

Talk to her.

And when he didn't call?

I didn't need to ask.

I knew.

COVID lockdown.

Or someone stepped out of line.

Didn't matter who.

They all paid.

They all sat in silence while the world outside just kept turning.

The journey to Clarence took three days. Enrico explained after he returned in December 2022, just how controlled and organized inmate transport is. He described how strict the rules are at every step, starting with getting the inmates into the vehicle, locking them in place, and making sure the truck is fully secured before it leaves. There are also rules on how long inmates can sit in certain positions, with planned breaks to make sure the journey doesn't become too harsh. Even talking to the inmates during the trip follows set rules to keep everyone safe. Enrico said it all seemed carefully planned to avoid problems and keep both the inmates and officers protected.

In short, what should've taken half a day took three long days. He said it was draining and cruel.

At Clarence Correctional Complex, inmates were given tablets and access to a special app. This app let them stay in touch with their families for a small fee, allowing them to call home anytime with no limit on how many times they called. This gave them a way to hold onto some sense of normal life, keeping their family ties alive while locked up.

When Enrico was first sent to Silverwater MRCC, he asked me to sign up for the prison's online system so I could send him money regularly. He told me he didn't go to the canteen much because it was full of tension and threats. The stronger inmates, called "kingpins," would often start trouble there, and it wasn't worth the risk for him. He avoided it so he wouldn't ruin his chance at bail. Instead, he skipped meals to stay out of harm's way.

Money also mattered because things were often stolen. Enrico would return to his cell to find his cupboard emptied, his food gone. Inmates could buy extra items, called "buy-ups," using money sent from outside. Enrico mostly bought cans of tuna, his most valued item.

Clarence Correctional Complex has its own economy, and a can of tuna, something that costs mere cents in a supermarket and is casually tossed into a shopping trolley, transformed into a highly sought-after commodity behind bars. In prison, a single small can of tuna could be exchanged for necessities such as one tablet of Panadol, a can of soft drink, a single band-aid, one roll of toilet paper, or even a bar of soap.

This transformation of mundane items into valuable currency highlighted the harsh conditions within the prison system and the limited resources available to inmates. It also revealed the incredible resourcefulness and adaptability of human nature as inmates navigated this parallel economy to meet their basic needs.

Witnessing this reality firsthand was an eye-opening experience for me. It was sobering to see how something we take for granted could become a vital lifeline for someone else. It brought into sharp focus the deprivations of life behind bars and the resilience required to survive in such an environment.

It was eye-opening, it was harsh, it didn't feel real.

Even while Enrico was inside, I kept sending him money to help him survive. I didn't want him to suffer more than he already was. I wanted justice, yes, but I also wanted to hold on to what made me human. I wasn't out for revenge - I just wanted things to be fair, and to keep my own values.

After Enrico was sent to Clarence, I moved out of the city to Norwest in Sydney, NSW. I took all of Enrico's things with me, packed them up, and stored them in the garage. I knew he'd need them when he came out, and I didn't want him to come back to nothing. Those boxes were my way of saying I hadn't given up completely. I was still willing to help him face what came next, even though we had both gone through so much.

Clarence Correctional Centre brought about a series of "reckoning" moments.

Enrico and I were on the phone. I asked, "Tell me, why are you in jail?"

Enrico replied, "Because you put me in here."

I pushed back, "No. No. No. Tell me why I did it?"

Enrico said, "I can't. I'm not alone."

He was referring to what he'd told me before – how inmates would report private conversations to the so-called "masculine" leaders of the block. They had zero tolerance for weak men begging women over the phone. Weak men were singled out and beaten in dark corners.

But I didn't back down.

"Enrico, tell me, why are you in jail?"

Enrico whispered, "Because I took your money."

"No," I said. "You're not in jail for that. I gave up on the money long ago. You're in jail because you objectified women. You've done it for years."

The next day, Enrico was reported beaten up by inmates.

There were many arguments.

There was a lot of anger.

There was also some acceptance.

There was screaming.

There was crying.

One day, Enrico called me out of the blue. His voice was tense, full of frustration and discomfort. He told me he had a splinter in his finger, and it had gotten badly infected. The pain was so bad he hadn't slept the night before.

The call came while I was at work, trying to keep everything together. I stepped out onto the balcony of my office in Norwest, just trying to get a quiet moment to focus on what he was saying.

"Okay," I said, trying to think of something useful. "You need something small and sharp," I added, picturing a needle, tweezers, or anything that might help him. I paced the balcony, listening as he described the swelling, the redness, the pain that wouldn't let him rest. He sounded tired. Worn down. And it wasn't just about a splinter – it was another problem he couldn't fix.

Then came the sigh.

"Narghiza, I'm in prison. There's nothing small or sharp here."

And that's when it hit me. Again.

How hard his life really was.

And how I was the cause of it.

There were nights when Enrico was restless, unable to sleep because of the pain, and he couldn't even get a single painkiller. He pressed the emergency button repeatedly, but no one showed up - not once during the entire night. He was left to deal with the pain alone.

Then there were nights when something as simple as a spider bite became unbearable. The swelling, the fever, the discomfort - it all dragged on through the night, and again, no one came to help. He spent those hours burning up, with nothing to ease the pain or lower the fever.

What hit hardest was the first AVL, the video meeting I finally agreed to after months of refusing to see him. I remember how nervous I was, unsure of what to expect. Just days earlier, I'd heard from his cellmate that Enrico had collapsed from a seizure. He'd passed out suddenly outside his cell and woke up in the clinic. His cellmate had called me, letting me know Enrico was recovering.

What I saw on the screen that day was horrifying. There wasn't a patch of skin on him that wasn't bruised or battered. Shades of pink, blue, and purple covered every bit of flesh I could see. He looked thinner, weaker. His hair was slicked back into a ponytail, and he seemed on edge the entire time. He spent the whole meeting showing me the bruises, rolling up his sleeves, pointing out every injury like he needed me to see it all, like he needed me to understand what he was going through. It was obvious - he was as nervous as I was, but also desperate to keep the conversation going.

The day he passed out was worse than I imagined. The prison had no tolerance for weakness, no patience for anyone who couldn't stand their ground - even those with serious medical conditions. When Enrico collapsed, he didn't just lose consciousness. While he was lying there, motionless, others kicked him. Repeatedly. Hard. Feet connected with his head, his chest, his stomach. They didn't care that he was already out cold. There were several inmates involved, surrounding him, kicking him as if he wasn't even human.

There were those who did the kicking. There were those who stood by and said nothing. And there were those who saw it all but stayed silent, afraid of what would happen if they spoke up. When the officers came to investigate, no one talked. No one stepped forward. The whole thing was closed, just like that.

After I wrote this, I let Enrico read the draft. These were my memories, shaped by what I heard and saw from the outside. But he lived it. What was memory for me was his reality for a long time.

I was expecting a reaction. We were sitting together in Bankstown Sports Club, Sydney, NSW, having a cup of coffee. For a moment, he was still - completely motionless, frozen in thought. I couldn't read his emotions. I watched him closely, waiting for something, anything, but there was just silence.

"It's okay not to have anything to say," I told him, though inside I felt a twinge of disappointment. I thought the chapter would stir something in him, spark a deeper response.

It did.

Enrico slowly began to tear up, the emotions creeping in, bit by bit. Then he looked at me, struggling to hold back the weight of everything he was feeling, and said, "The chapter doesn't even touch the surface of what I've been through." His voice cracked, and the tears came harder. He cried for a while, still raw from that part of his life, the one that had left the deepest, most tormenting scars - scars that hadn't faded, even now.

He had so many memories to share. But the one that stood out, the one he kept coming back to, was his memory of seeing me on AVL, the first video meeting after months of pleading with me, waiting for me to finally agree. That moment meant everything to him.

Enrico's Recollection of The Day snd Events After

The entire block knew that I had marital issues. After swapping through three cellmates, I ended up with one who regularly ratted out my conversations with Narghiza. His behaviour made it clear that he wanted to be in the cell while I was on the phone with her. At Clarence Correctional Complex, there were inmate-imposed behavioural codes, and one of them was that cellmates gave each other privacy during phone calls by stepping out to the yard. My current cellmate didn't follow that code. He didn't have anyone on the outside who cared to speak to him, so he stayed.

As if eavesdropping wasn't enough, he would throw in passing comments during my calls with Narghiza, almost as if he was joining the conversation himself. But it didn't stop there. Whatever I said to Narghiza would inevitably be twisted and repeated to others in the block. It would come back distorted, designed to make me look weak and to get me in trouble with the tougher inmates. The block had no time for men they saw as soft - no time for the ones they called damp tissues stuck to the heel of a wife's shoe.

The block knew I was trying to save my marriage. They knew I had cheated before and that I was paying the price. They knew Narghiza wasn't happy with me. They heard her hang up on me, call me names, refuse to come to AVL for months. They knew she was my weakness.

The block came with its own ecosystem of rules, codes, behaviours, and its own lifestyle. The block had its own red carpet, and inmates who got to walk it were the luckiest and most fulfilled inmates on the block. The red-carpet walk wasn't just an act of putting one foot in front of the other. The walk on the red-carpet walk was worth more than any commodity circulating in the block's undercover exchange system. The red-carpet walk was a journey to "Hope Island." It was like a second lease in life for those afflicted with a terminal disease; it's like getting access to compatible organs that are one-in-a-million match. It's like being told that soon, once the transplant occurred, I would be able to walk and talk again. I would breathe, smell fresh air, laugh, and cry like everybody else on the outside. No, Clarence's red carpet wasn't walking; it was stepping into a future.

It led inmates to the AVL rooms, where they met their loved ones on the screen for the entire 30 minutes once a week.

Walking on the red carpet were not celebrities. Or celebrities of their own kind. These celebrities are better classed as gladiators marching to the grand arena of an emotional battlefield that could end up being their last fight. Time and time again, I saw inmates come out of the AVL rooms with devastating news, their loved ones did not want to see or be associated with them anymore. I genuinely did not know what was less evil not to know that your family was not waiting for you anymore or to know and be told that was the case.

A Case of Trevor

As my life hung by a thin thread with Narghiza, I watched my friend-inmate Trevor get rejected on the phone by his partner. She told him never to call her again. I witnessed firsthand what losing hope looked like.

Trevor was incarcerated for substance abuse. He was a high-end Italian chef with Lebanese roots. The only thing that kept Trevor clean was the precious hope of redeeming himself - getting clean and proving his worth to his partner and their young daughter. That hope was all he had. Only if...

After that call, Trevor spent the day searching for internal dealers, unable to process the rejection. He spiralled, retreating into himself. Days later, I saw him again, but the Trevor I knew was gone. He was buried deep within the distant, dilated retinas of his eyes. There was nothing I could do for him without risking drawing the guards' attention. Involving them meant more charges, more time.

I stood there for a while, staring at the photo of Trevor's happy face, thinking. Thinking of a lot of things. I thought of Narghiza and what she said a few days ago. "Some choices we make as human beings reflect the circumstantial selection from degrees of evils." When you're faced with tough choices and none of them offer peace, let alone something right, you're forced to choose the lesser of the evils in front of you.

On the phone, she had screamed at me that she rescued me from something far worse. She said one day I'd thank her for what she had done. I wasn't sure if this - what I was seeing unfold in front of me - was what she meant. A man's life spiralling out of control, and all I could do was stand by, watch in agony, or "rescue" him by adding another three to five years to his sentence.

I cried. In silence.

Substance abuse was not an option I ever entertained while I bore the unrelenting weight of a brutal, humiliating truth - Narghiza's headstrong refusal to see me on the AVL. Her rejection was a dagger twisted in wounds already festering, deepened by the ruthless reality of my confinement. The fallout of my desperate attempts to persuade her led not just to scorn but to violence, as my own cellmate betrayed me, sparking fierce clashes with others who dared linger too close.

I drowned my anguish in the salt of my tears, mingling with the sorrow of those cursed by similarly grim fates. The universe seemed infinitely cruel, a pitiless orchestrator revelling in my torment, withholding even the smallest mercy as I spiralled into the bleakest abyss of despair. Narghiza's refusal to meet me on the AVL did not seem like a rescue. It felt like rejection. It felt like the final stone cast at me when I was already completely shattered.

No doubt, inmates were placing bets on my marriage, with some beyond confident that Narghiza would not book an AVL, and even if she did, she would ghost me. Others believed that time heals it all and that with the daily telephone communication between me and her, we had a high chance of getting to see each other and possibly recovering our marriage down the track.

Inmate speculations added to my growing anxieties. There were days I wished my sentence had been death by hanging. In twisted moments of clarity, I imagined how that rope might have saved me from the crushing weight of false hopes - the desperate, delusional belief that someone, anyone, would wait for me, would care if I ever walked free again. Perhaps it would have been a mercy, sparing me the torment of this hollow existence.

I even found myself clinging to the thought of purpose in death - donating my organs to those more deserving of life than I could ever claim to be. But even that noble idea darkened. My mind spiralled to selling my organs instead, to repay debts I had no hope of settling otherwise. I pictured the faces of those I owed, their resentment melting into reluctant acceptance.

Forgiveness?

No, forgiveness was too much to ask, too much of a dream for someone like me. I never dared to envision forgiving faces. That would have been a kindness I knew I didn't deserve.

A Case of Anthony

Anthony had brain damage. That's how I met him, through his access to Panadol. He was a vibrant guy, full of life despite the cruel reality of his condition. Yet, his mental state was a glaring reminder of the system's failure. Why was Anthony here, in Clarence, a prison, instead of the medical institution where he belonged? The answer didn't make sense then, and it still doesn't.

Anthony was a prisoner within a prison. His fragile state made him a target, vulnerable to violence. Outside the thin walls of his cell, his life was always at risk. So, he stayed confined, locking himself away as if he could quarantine the world's brutality. Voluntarily. It was survival, but at what cost?

I couldn't help but think of the documentary I once saw about factory farming of chickens on steroids. It exposed the horrors of caged chickens, packed so tightly they couldn't move, denied the space to act on their natural instincts. Overcrowding turned them into something grotesque, aggressive, cannibalistic, de-evolved versions of themselves, twisted by sheer desperation to survive.

Anthony was no different. His confinement bred its own mutations. His mind fractured further under the weight of isolation, a harsh side effect of self-imposed captivity. This wasn't just survival, it was a slow, inescapable collapse of humanity, all because the world outside his cell was far more dangerous than the prison inside it.

After I got released from Clarence, I helped Anthony by looking after the only soul that awaited him outside his cell – his dog Cleo. I looked after Cleopatra for several months. I was proud to return her to Anthony when he got discharged, though Anthony was no longer equipped to deal with freedom, spaces, liberties or people. Not long after his release, he was reported to have been back in incarceration. I did not try to find out what happened to Cleo. I found it too painful to pursue answers.

My dramatic prison life was interrupted one day.

Suddenly.

Narghiza declared she was booking me for an AVL. It happened after I was released from the prison hospital. Days before her declaration, I woke up in the hospital after being brutally beaten by inmates while I was unconscious on the floor.

Miraculously and unexpectedly, I got to walk the red carpet. The walk was surreal. The journey on the red carpet walks you past the cells on the block. Privacy in the block is non-existent. Well, before you get to know you have an AVL, rumours float that you are going to have an AVL. Your entire journey on the red carpet is filled with inmates posing themselves in a line, ready to shake your hand, nudge you on the shoulder, and bang their metal mugs against metal to create a prison "cheer noise." All the while screaming, "Pucci!"

"Pucci!"

"Pucci!"

I was very nervous meeting Narghiza. She looked concerned and focused on my scars and bruises. I was so keen to maintain the conversation that I immediately subconsciously kicked in with my sales pitch constructed entirely on show and tell of the dents, scars, and bruises. Narghiza had no idea how little those wounds meant to me compared to the far deeper soul-destroying thoughts and fears I had of losing her. Losing us. Losing hope.

From that point on, I saw Narghiza every week for some two months until my release from prison.

A few days before my release, I met with my lawyer. He had prepared the release documents, which stated that I would be residing with my father. When I informed him that I wanted to change that, to reside with my wife, Narghiza Ergashova, he paused, clearly taken aback. His expression, a mix of disbelief and concern, said it all: "Are you out of your mind? Have you completely lost it?" Though the questions remained unspoken, their weight filled the room. After a moment of silence, he simply responded, "As you wish," and assured me he would amend the release documents shortly. He did.

Prison taught me a profound truth: the people in our lives are our most genuine connections and the only possessions that truly matter, built through shared memories. It's ironic how little time we make for one another in the outside world. We chase fleeting, often obscure goals that rise and fall repeatedly, all the while taking the most valuable aspects of our lives, our families and friends, for granted.

Prison taught me that every journey I make back to my wife after my day job is a walk on the red carpet towards my trophy - the only trophy that matters - my family.

Prison taught me that my wife was right. Not all choices are the kind that pit "best" against "better." Choices are far more complex, far more visceral. The true weight of a decision isn't measured by the option chosen but by the fire that fuels it. Was it born of love, destitution, fury or anger and revenge?

The truth is the prison wasn't just a consequence; it was salvation cloaked in iron bars. To me, it was the crucible that burned away pretences, leaving me to face the raw, unforgiving truths of who I was and who I could have become if I channelled myself in the right direction.

Prison was my necessary evil.

Curly Clux Convictions

Is incarceration truly the path to transformation, or does it simply perpetuate a cycle of punishment by creating more troubled recidivists? Opinions on this topic remain deeply divided, with some believing in its rehabilitative potential, while others argue it fails to address the issue in its entirety.

However, here are some glaring statistics from the US:

1. High Recidivism Rates:

- A 2021 Bureau of Justice Statistics study found that 66% of individuals released from prison in 24 states in 2008 were re-arrested within three years, and 82% were re-arrested within a decade.
- Rearrest rates for those released in 2012 remained high, with 71% being rearrested within five years.

2. Reincarceration:

1. 61% of prisoners released in 2008 returned to prison within a decade due to parole violations, probation violations, or new sentences.

3. Employment and Housing Barriers:

- Around 60% of formerly incarcerated individuals remain unemployed a year after release. Background checks revealing criminal records significantly reduce job opportunities, with callbacks or job offers decreasing by 50%.
- Homelessness is up to 11 times more likely among formerly incarcerated individuals, further increasing the likelihood of reoffending.

4. Systemic Failures:

- The U.S. criminal justice system is criticized for over-punishing and under-rehabilitating individuals, creating a cycle of reoffending.
- Technical violations, such as missing a check-in or breaking house arrest rules, often lead to reincarceration.

5. Youth and Crime:

Younger individuals are more likely to re-offend, with those released at age 24 or younger being 64% more likely to return to prison within five years compared to those aged 40 or older.

6. Global Comparison:

- The U.S. has the highest recidivism rates globally, partly due to longer prison sentences and fewer rehabilitation-focused programs compared to countries like those in Scandinavia.

These statistics highlight the systemic challenges and barriers faced by formerly incarcerated individuals, which often perpetuate cycles of crime and incarceration.

In contrast, there is mounting evidence suggesting that recovery from health-related issues is fast-tracked if loving family and friends surround the patient. This leads to:

1. Improved Health Outcomes:

- Individuals with strong social and emotional support are less likely to die from health conditions like cardiovascular disease and depression.
- Social support reduces stress, which is linked to better immunity and lower risks of heart disease.

2. Faster Recovery:

- Emotional support from loved ones helps individuals cope better with stress and trauma, reducing the likelihood of disorders like PTSD.
- Instrumental support, like help with daily tasks or meals, speeds up physical recovery.

3. Behavioral Benefits:

- Social groups encourage healthier behaviors, such as quitting smoking or maintaining a balanced diet, which can accelerate recovery.

4. Mental Health and Resilience:

- People with strong social networks feel more capable of handling challenges, contributing to faster psychological recovery.

5. Substance Recovery:

- Studies show that greater social support predicts lower substance use rates, better treatment retention, and higher abstinence self-efficacy.

Hard evidence showing how support and reintegration efforts improve outcomes for prisoners post-release:

1. Family Contact During Incarceration:

- Maintaining family contact during incarceration reduces recidivism by 30.7%.
- Family contact improves mental health and post-release adjustment, as it fosters connectedness and helps with reintegration planning.

2. Employment and Vocational Training:

- Stable employment is key to reducing recidivism. Programs like EMPLOY reduced recidivism by 32-55% and increased employment rates by 72% within a year of release.
- Work release programs, such as Florida's Work Release Program, showed participants were 4-10% less likely to reoffend and five times more likely to secure employment.

3. Supportive Housing:

- Programs like Returning Home Ohio (RHO) provide affordable housing with integrated support services. Participants were 40% less likely to be arrested and 61% less likely to be reincarcerated compared to non-participants.

4. Behavioral Health and Cognitive Behavioral Therapy (CBT):

- CBT and therapeutic communities help address mental health and substance use, reducing recidivism.
- For example, the Amity In-Prison Therapeutic Community program reduced reincarceration and improved employment outcomes.

5. Comprehensive Reentry Programs:

- Programs like the InnerChange Freedom Initiative, which combine mentorship, family support, and community service preparation, significantly reduced rearrest and reconviction rates.

These findings underscore the importance of structured support systems, including family connections, employment opportunities, housing, and behavioural health services, in helping formerly incarcerated individuals reintegrate successfully into society.

Within Australian society, there exists no single "framework" that provides former inmates with any form of naturalisation. Some inmates are expected to be integrated into the community after a decade-long incarceration, having no skills or coping mechanisms to catch up on the insurmountable amount of hi-tech development the human race has gone through. They are confronted with a new sense of fashion, new lingo, new phones, new thoughts, new concepts, comprehend AI, how scammers work nowadays, and who is considered a real scammer now because everyone looks and acts like one. It is a daunting world to return to.

Enrico Pucci spent eight months finding his feet after his incarceration. On Sundays, he attended Hill Song Church in Hills District, walked the dog of a fellow inmate, and helped me with running my life and my business. He was timid for the first few months. Unsure of things. Having little confidence in himself.

Enrico obtained his first consultancy work in August 2023 within an Australian company. He glitzed through it.

In April 2025, Enrico stepped into a pivotal consultancy role as a Vice President of Sales and Development for Asia Pacific Region with a leading global organization. Tasked with overseeing a network of prisons across the region, Enrico was handpicked for his vision and "expertise" as a former inmate seeking to improve conditions and post-release rehabilitation of inmates. His mission was nothing short of transformative: to implement and uphold humane business practices that redefined the tendering processes and drove measurable improvements in the relationships between inmates and prison personnel.

By the time this manuscript was completed, Enrico had 12 out of 13 merit points available on his driver's licence. He was fighting for the remaining 1 point in the local court in Sydney, NSW. Besides, he had a full-time driver and a bodyguard. He had no need to drive.

He has not obtained debt or signed up for any form of debt facility, including a credit card.

Enrico was domiciled outside of Australia and was no longer an Australian resident for tax purposes.

Can Enrico sustain it long-term?

Only time can tell.

I, on the other hand, have been extremely lucky to have had my healing. It's been a privilege to witness Enrico's journey this far. There are many places I could have been right now. But my truth is I am happy exactly where I am.

I am Enrico Pucci's wife.

In getting to this point, Enrico endured years of digital and physical harassment and humiliation imposed by his ex-partner of 90 days, Dina Aslan. It seemed getting the harshest penalty in the roughest prison was not enough for Dina.

In April 2023, Dina sent hitmen debt collectors to our residence.

The gesture was followed by a visit from an Australian Current Affair in July 2023.

Dina took up blogging as Lady Whistleblow, in which she seemingly unravelled the truth in the triangular dynamic that she disturbingly believed existed, completely unaware just how many chapters she was off the actual position of truth and acceptance.

She sent threatening letters wrapped as promotional material to our address.

She harassed my daughter, Shirina Holmatova. My friends and my colleagues.

She harassed Enrico's daughter, Chiara Masstroianni; Enrico's ex-wife, Belinda, had to file for a Personal Violence Order against Dina.

Dina passionately portrayed us as an organised crime network in her blog. In it, all Puccis managed to not only talk - which was not the case - but also meaningfully arrange themselves in such a manner where they could plan and "organise crimes." The nature of the crimes varied from blog to blog.

She then went on claiming in the next blog that despite us Puccis being the criminals, she was the one pulled up by police 39 times in the past 5 years, plus one arrest and release the following day.

She called these visits "vexatious" allegations.

In none of these actions did Dina see the humour or the humiliation she was putting herself through.

The definition of "truth" employed in Dina Aslan's version of events is outside the scope of this manuscript.

Curly Flix and Chicks - Do Pink Pigs Fly?

Dina and Enrico met on RSVP, a dating site. Dina gave Enrico 500,000 AUD. The question here is whether it is feasible that a middle-aged "Cinderella" meets her middle-aged "Prince Charming" on RSVP and becomes so swept off her feet that she engages in conversations warranting the exchange of an extraordinarily large sum - half a million dollars - on day 68 of a 90-day relationship?

The only documented evidence supporting this exchange is a few text messages between the parties. The final message from Aslan to Pucci reads, "No problem habibi. You would have done the same thing for me."

In other words, the question remains: Do pink pigs really fly?

My understanding is that Dina Jamil Hamdi Aslan (Ms. Aslan, from here on) and Enrico Pucci (Enrico, from here on) were involved in an alleged romantic and/or business partnership between the 6th of September 2020 and the 7th of December 2020.

It is fair to say that, given the conflicting reports, the true nature and purpose of this brief association remain undefined.

It is also understood that innumerable documents have been submitted to Australian Courts, NSW Police, and other legal authorities, with ever-shifting timelines regarding the start and end of the purported "relationship." These dates appear to change from statement to statement, depending on their propensity to attain the "golden fleece" of restitution sought.

Thus, I cautiously note that the initial online connection likely commenced on or around May 2020, characterized by open dating, with both parties - Enrico and Dina - engaging in multiple romantic liaisons simultaneously. The nature of this "connection," whether it was commercial or romantic, was, therefore, open to broad interpretation.

It is my understanding that physical, non-exclusive dating with intense sexual exchanges, including written and verbal sexual innuendos, began on the 6th of September 2020 and ended on the 7th of December 2020 - a total of 90 days.

Reviewing Aslan's initial statement of claim (2020/00363301), according to Aslan, the short-lived 90-day "connection" involved an alleged multi-million dollar commitment - $10 million, to be precise - in the form of property located at Unit 2604, Kent Street, Millers Point. The following contributions were alleged to have been made by both parties:

- **Enrico Pucci** – 100%
- **Dina Aslan** – 0% (a loan of $0.5 million to be fully repaid after the purchase of the property)

The nature of the loan, as described, resembles a personal loan, which strengthens Aslan's claim that she sought marriage with Enrico. However, no evidence exists to support this claim, aside from Dina's verbal assertions.

Going over the submissions and transcripts of the ADVO case no. 2023/00312512, held on the 29th of November 2023 and the 13th of December 2023, it becomes clear that Aslan's claims shifted over time. In these particular hearings, she stated that the half a million dollars she gave Enrico was to enter a business and run a production company with him called Curly Flix and Chicks.

A key point here: Enrico had no experience in the entertainment industry.

Yet, the funding breakdown for this alleged venture looked like this:

- **Enrico Pucci** – 0%
- **Dina Aslan** – $500,000 AUD

The nature of this loan now resembled a business loan, where love and romance seemingly had nothing to do with the transaction. It became a commercial deal - at least according to her latest submissions.

But submission after submission, Ms. Aslan's claims shifted, depending on what angle served her best. Her arguments were built on her personal view of events, which dramatically changed each time.

- On one hand, she showed an unusual willingness to believe unlikely stories, as long as they worked in her favour, even when there was no evidence to back them up.
- On the other hand, she demonstrated an almost fanatic commitment to research, insisting on its accuracy, again, as long as it worked for her.

Yet, none of her submissions addressed the real issue - the moral hazard.

The question remains:

Under what circumstances did a woman, on the most charitable visa in Australia - Refugee / Subclass 866 Under Protection by the Australian Government - end up having access to and freely distributing such large sums of cash?

Let's be clear:

For a fraction of that amount - $100,000 USD - Dina could have secured full citizenship in the island nation of Vanuatu, without enduring 5 to 10 years of Australian immigration processing.

So, who was she running from, if anyone?

And how did she access and transfer such large amounts internationally, bringing them into Australia without declaring them or paying taxes?

How did she receive workers' compensation subsidies in Australia, while sitting on so much money, actively seeking both business ventures and romantic liaisons online?

This manuscript will not dive deeper into whether or not "Pink Pigs Fly."

It's not here to get lost in the fantasy of Curly Flix and Chicks, full of conviction and zero evidence.

Instead, what follows are Dina Aslan's own explanations, given to me, about why she chose to date and pursue an emotionally unavailable man like Enrico.

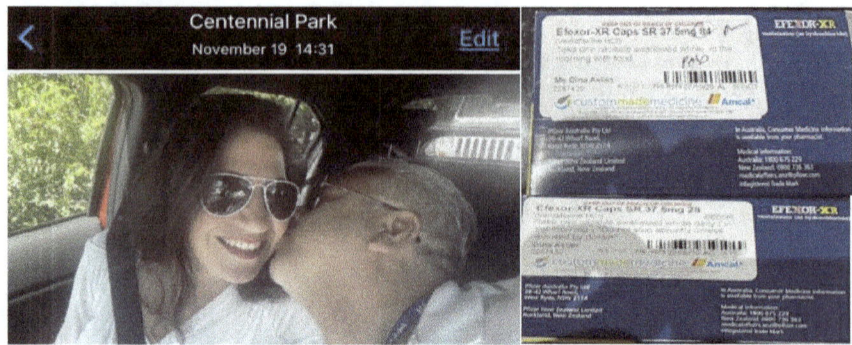

The image of Aslan was taken on 19th of Nov 2020 (as featured in Australian Current Affair) and dates on the psychotropic medications dispensed under her name dated June and October 2020 - Dina was on Workers Compensation subsidy that deemed her unfit to work.

Below are a series (non-exhaustive) of barbaric messages Aslan sent me to explain why she went on being intimate with Enrico, knowing that he did not appear emotionally available nor single.

Dated 27th of October 2021 at 07:19:58 AM AEDT

"for example, you mentioned something about 3rd of December, which stupidly made me check my phone for that day. Ifound a FaceTime call from him which means that we had phone sex that day with you sleeping in his bed. And that wasn"t the only time…"

Dated 28th of October 2021 at 06:44:21 AM AEDT

"When I saw you on his social media, he claimed that you and him have an arrangement where you pretended to be together so that he can reduce the child support amount being paid to the extorting ex-wife (Belinda) who was by then demanding $10,000 a week as he claimed. He said you were a jobless Russian that needed the $400 that he pays you to pose as an aenagged partner."

Dated 25th of October 2021 at 02:12:57 PM AEDT

"He kept attempting to convience me that you were some Russian trash who pimped her own daigher under her own roof and that it ws when he heard your daughter having sex with different guys and different times that he knew you will never have a motherly label towards Chiara…"

Curly Flix and Chicks, The Keyboard Production

From the second week of April 2023 to date, I remain the sole subject of vicious, calculated cyber terror attacks instigated by Aslan in retaliation for her failed romantic liaison with my husband, then estranged fiancé, Enrico Pucci.

The full extent of Aslan's cyber terrorism acts is not known, nor can it be qualified or qualified without draining resources to prove the obvious - Aslan has targeted me to cause me deliberate harm; otherwise, using her words put to me in an email in December 2020, "to destroy me."

Aslan used sophisticated, illegal cyber-scraping bots to access the personal information of my friends, family, wider network, and complete strangers.

Specifically, Aslan was scrapping their contact details to share her website and promote her "misleading investigative work," according to which, in some of her communication, I had to be arrested for reasons of and accusations I find paralysing, groundless, offensive.

The use of illegal cyber-scraping bots by Aslan to access personal information was in clear violation of privacy and is considered a form of cyber terrorism.

Aslan's actions are not only unethical but downright illegal. Her misguided attempts to exert influence and manipulate individuals to harm me through the use of personal information are highly alarming and pose a serious threat to the security of those involved, as well as mine.

Aslan's attacks involved an elaborate setup. The setup is mind-boggling and a true testament to the sick nature of the person Aslan stands for. The setup involves the four online personas fully orchestrated by Aslan herself. The role of each persona is described below.

Aslan's Google Profile – "Ladywhistleblow"

Aslan operates a Google profile and website under the name "Ladywhistleblow," which she uses to publish slanderous content about me in an attempt to tarnish my reputation through Google search results.

The website employs highly illegal methods to manipulate search engine visibility, including:

- **BOT Boosting**: Hundreds of fake Google profiles are set up to artificially search for my name and visit Aslan's website. This tricks Google's algorithm into believing there is genuine interest and organic traffic, thereby boosting the site's ranking in search results.

- **Latching and Hooking**: Aslan's website aggressively uses hyperlinking to attach itself to my personal content, creating false associations that increase her site's visibility whenever someone searches for my initials or related terms.

These tactics are not only unethical but may also violate cybercrime laws regarding defamation, impersonation, and the use of bots to manipulate search engine rankings.

Aslan takes herself to ACA because her website won't rank or be taken seriously without a third-party authority, and that comes with a high authority score website.

Aslan links her website to all Channel 9 electronic publications to give herself a valid voice that people are compelled to trust, but she also boosts her website on Google through serious front linking.

Aslan's LinkedIn alias – Sandy Bell. The website sitting idle in Google SERP (search engine result pages) does not do enough damage.

If Aslan were to destroy me, as her plan was, she needs her content delivered to the target audience – my work colleagues, business, and professional network.

Fake profile called Sandy Bell was set up to harvest connections in LinkedIn, that is, target connections. Bulk of Sandy Bell's connections were my current and ex-colleagues and employers on LinkedIn.

Once connected, Sandy Bell gains access to the email addresses of LinkedIn users. This allows Sandy Bell not only to promote Ladywhistleblow content via LinkedIn InMails, but also to harvest personal - often professional - email addresses. These addresses are then fed into the Ladywhistleblow website's system, enabling the sending of unsolicited, slanderous material to individuals outside of LinkedIn.

Several of my colleagues have reported receiving degrading, slut-shaming, and court-tendered materials about me. These messages were delivered both through the Sandy Bell LinkedIn account and directly to their personal and professional email accounts. Many of these individuals were shocked, expressing confusion as to how Ladywhistleblow obtained their private contact details.

These practices are strictly prohibited in Australia:

- LinkedIn bans the use of fake profiles and does not allow the creation of duplicate accounts.
- Under ACCC regulations, a company registered in Australia can face fines of up to $220,000 AUD for sending a single unsolicited promotional email.

However, Ladywhistleblow's website is not registered in Australia. It is registered in the United States, yet the primary operations and target audience are clearly Australian.

These actions constitute breaches of privacy laws, defamation, and potentially criminal telecommunications offences, especially as they involve unauthorised access to personal data and distribution of harmful content across international digital platforms.

Affecting my professional network would only eliminate a fraction of my followers on LinkedIn. The number of my following hovers around 175,000. It is not enough to render me unemployed, I must be destroyed and erased completely.

Hence, Aslan creates another profile on LinkedIn – Samad Shah.

This profile is dedicated to bullying me and targeting anyone who interacts with my content. Specifically, individuals who leave comments on my posts are subjected to harassment and degrading responses from a user operating under the name Samad Shah.

The Samad Shah profile regularly posts defamatory counter-comments, often hyperlinking to the *Ladywhistleblow* website, effectively promoting Dina Aslan's blog while attacking me and my network.

Among the comments left by this profile:

- I am referred to as a "wife of a criminal".
- There are statements implying that I will "be arrested soon for unspecified crimes".
- The profile demands that I "withdraw [my] defamation claim", using intimidation and slander as pressure tactics.

This profile operates relentlessly and in real-time, launching attacks immediately after any comment appears on my posts. These actions constitute malicious, targeted harassment.

Such behaviour is not only in violation of LinkedIn's policies - which strictly prohibit harassment, bullying, and spreading misinformation - but also falls under telecommunications offences, as it involves the use of carrier services to cause harm. These actions are illegal and subject to criminal prosecution.

My Personal Conviction

My position started at "Cracking The Code – Take One". The code was solely focused on the Pucci brothers. And I was the victim, just like the other lovers. The code was missing a deeper "exploration" of the characters surrounding the Pucci brothers, especially the wild card figure – Dina Aslan herself.

I have since moved to "Take Three". In my view, not only each case must be explored on its own merit, but also a question must be raised as to who exploited whom and for what purpose in every scenario.

It is particularly so in the case of Dina Aslan.

I found ways to restore my inner balance and courage to forgive Enrico.

I sincerely hope that one day, Dina finds the courage to forgive herself.